Bizarre Messaging //
Joey Del Duca

Bizarre Messaging

Cover and book design by Joey Del Duca

@joeydelduca
joeydelducaauthor@gmail.com
joeydelduca.com

Author photo by John Sancho

ISBN: 9781703187373

#0 – The Ropes Wrapped Around His Hands (10.26.19)

Matthew adjusted the way the ropes wrapped around his hands, now nearly blistered to the bone, and pulled his cargo forward, one man expected to exert the power of a mule, through mountain and valley, just for a mere sample.

After an hour he stopped for a break. He looked up at the sun, the skin around his squinted eyes chapped and darkened from this endless journey.

He pulled out the locket with her face inside, all he needed to persevere, and carried on.

#1 – A Single Soulless Structure (1.18.19)

Junior played with his building blocks on the living room floor. Despite his focus and attention to detail on his craft, his main preoccupation fell on Frank, who sat on the couch watching the TV with beer in hand, laughing mindlessly at whatever transpired on the screen.

Junior placed a green block on his current project, a single soulless structure, blank as a child fresh in the world.

"Unbelievable," Frank muttered at the woman on the TV, then took a swig of beer.

#2 – Dirty Package (1.19.19)

The package felt disgusting in her hands as she walked down the sidewalk.

Perhaps it was its source, the homeless messenger. At least she assumed he was homeless. She couldn't be sure if anything was as it seemed anymore, not since her involvement in whatever this was had begun, maybe four months ago. Before that, she was just another young woman trying to make it in modern America.

#3 – "They" (1.19.19)

None of the captives knew what they were being fed during any given meal, they were just appreciative for anything They put before them, whoever "They" were. Only the one showed himself to them, the large black one with a face as solid and stern as a slab of concrete until they began eating, when he smiled to reveal two rows of rotting teeth.

They had all been conditioned to starve, to lose all concept of empty desire and personal preference. They would eat and he would smile as they chewed and swallowed the meat.

#4 – Community Leader and Protector (1.19.19)

Demmel sat tense in the back of the classroom. That Miss

Ramon could act as though she hadn't snitched him out to Hartshorn only yesterday, now so lighthearted before the classroom, as interested in entertaining her students as passing along the knowledge of the course, Contemporary Anthropology, moved something inside him.

She'd taught Demmel all he needed to know about her and her false role as community leader and protector. If she cared one pound worth of truth about protection, she wouldn't have placed a target on his back.

#5 – Wide-Winged Chaos Baring Its Fangs (1.19.19)

----

[1]

Andrebis sat upon his throne of bone, his eyes glowing red in the darkness of his chamber, his form reduced to a regal silhouette burnt into the crimson field emanating from his eyes, surpassing the will of the shadows.

The girl of the night groveled on the stone floor before his altar. Whatever

words she spoke fell upon deaf ears, which had been ground to blurred beacons of once mortal senses after the centuries of his evolution.

All he could understand was the fearful shaking of her form.

[2]

"I'm here for you," she said to the floor.

He did not care for her feelings, for the reasons of her individual presence. Those whose assistance he depended on, his beholden, had delivered this gift, that was all that mattered.

Children of yesterday sworn to duty into tomorrow, carrying the burdens and traditions of their forbearers.

Born to feed him, to secure his sustained detachment from society for time immemorial.

She took a chance to look up, finding the bottomless vacuum of his eyes.

[3]

"Will you regard me?" she asked, her face folded into

the layers of her longing for acceptance, to feel present where she knelt before him before the moment he would consume her, exchange her blood and life for death and the beyond.

Andrebis's face went unchanged and the girl looked down, fearing that she would be chastised for breaking decorum. He exhaled deeply, a final gesture of his indifference.

Then he came down upon her, wide-winged chaos sinking its fangs into the flesh of the sacrifice.

#6 – Chorus of Holiday Joy (1.19.19)

The men voiced a chorus of holiday joy as they danced about the ballroom, doing their best to prevent beer from overflowing their mugs.

Dollars Tatum, the barkeep, smiled widely as he watched the beer escape the patrons' stoups.

They were soldiers, yet the blood drying on their sleeves presented the end of battle for quite some time, based on the latest developments from headquarters.

Though they were built for war, no battle could arise when all enemies had already been vanquished.

#7 – Sloppy Joe Juices (1.20.19)

Billy watched Becky eat her dinner, beside himself with disgust. Regardless of her undeniable beauty, this date had plummeted below the bottom.

"Mmm, this is so good," she crooned, both elbows planted on the table, the sloppy Joe held in both hands, its juices dripping down her well-pointed chin, particles of bread lodged between her teeth. "Have you been here often? This is my first time."

"I have," he said, posture rigid, back not touching the chair.

#8 – Soothing Element (1.20.19)

"I don't know how much more of this I can take," Vishna whispered into the phone with the intensity of a scream. "He's wretched, disgusting. Being around him makes life unbearable. His smell sinks into your skin."

Ramos grunted contemplatively, voice low and gravely even when not conveying words. "Think of the future, my pet," he said finally, his voice casting its soothing element over her frayed nerves.

"I'll try," she said, eyes closed tight. "But for how long I do not know."

#9 – Breaking the Broken (1.20.19)

Kensu pounded his sledge onto the steel wedge, sending sparks into the darkening twilight. After several more swings, the concrete split and hung from the rusted reinforcement wire. He stepped back as the pile of rubble shifted, offsetting the wedge platform. He set the platform at a new point and beat it until the slab broke once more. On the cycle persisted, the senseless action of dismantling the

destroyed, that the broken could be further broken.

#10 – Each Presentation She Concocted to Conjure Their Interest (1.20.19)

Wendy stirred the lemonade suggestively with her ladle, but none of the workers paid any mind; such an indiscretion would provoke an inescapable punishment from the boss.

To the men, the worst of it was that she was unaware of the threat she invited with each presentation she concocted to conjure their interest.

"The juice is ready if any of y'all want a taste," she invited with her smooth Southern twang.

None of the men answered.

She smiled. "It's on the table if any of y'all change your mind."

#11 – Bad Kids (1.20.19)

Santa returned from his night exhausted, begrudgingly

rewarding the good ones from dusk till dawn.

Doesn't get easier with age, he thought to himself.

He closed the door before making his way down into the dungeon, where all the bad kids who had no one to keep them in line were kept.

"Hello, my little nasties," he greeted the imprisoned legions with his most festive exuberance. "Is everybody ready for their slops?"

They sat and watched, their hands on the bars.

#12 – Showdown at Memory Square (1.20.19)

Joyce stood where the opposing factions converged at the intersection of Memory Square. Despite having applied no allegiance to either side, fate would not discriminate.

Dozens of uninitiated citizens such as herself had been pushed into the nefarious middle ground, which would soon be trampled into yesterday.

Vision-obscuring glaciers of smoke blanketed everywhere Joyce looked.

Pipe bombs sounded in the distance, vacant of police presence.

#13 – Shadow Altar (1.20.19)

Laying on his belly, Morgan looked through the warehouse's window roof as the ceremony commenced within.

He promised Desiree he would do something, but what? The group, whatever they were called, possessed more power than he could comprehend.

Inside, on an altar in the shadows, stood a group of hooded men, who he assumed to be the elders, in rapt attention; their sacrifice lay strapped to an ancient stone slab, clad in a fur bikini.

"And so we have gathered."

#14 – Wolves in Human Form (1.20.19)

Eberle had never known the need to flee before. Instead he

was more prone to run directly into an explosion, finding great joy in adversity. But the tides were bound to change, and they did.

Eberle felt as though he were retreating from a legion of wolves in human form. He dared not turn around, it would only slow him down. So his legs kept pumping.

He ignored the growing pain as he crossed properties, running blindly, miraculously avoiding the limbs of trees as they tested him with their rigid reach.

#15 – The Wall of the Ice Cube (1.22.19)

Walla looked through the wall of the ice cube that encapsulated her like a prison. She couldn't move anything but her eyes, which somehow maintained their mobility; if only the rest of her body could move with such freedom.

Spectators circled the cube, riddled with a curiosity that seemed never to fade since the discovery of Walla and her cube so many years ago, her beauty and figure

perfectly preserved since the Doctor found her buried in the glacier.

#16 – Innocent Conversational Gesture (1.23.19)

For each time Greg watched Evan touch the hand of his wife, Stella—an innocent conversational gesture, no doubt—, he imagined driving his fork through the amiable man's hand.

Greg didn't care that the purpose of the dinner was to win Evan's confidence. Bianca, Evan's wife, looked anywhere but at the occupants of the circular table; clearly she had been in such situations before.

But not Greg.

"Evan, can we please have a word in private?"

#17 – Red with Glory (1.23.19)

The branch swayed in the wind, yet the crows that rowed its length found no reason to flee. Hanging by a rope tied to the branch, wrapped in a cotton pillowcase, Evan's head bobbed in sensitive response to that same wind.

The sky seemed red with glory to Greg, who stood on the tall grasses of the ground below, his arms wrapped over Bianca's shoulders.

"Well this is new," Bianca said, a cigarette hanging in her mouth.

Stella writhed at the base of the tree, blindfolded and gagged, her wrists bound by a rope behind the tree.

#18 – Toward the Stars (1.24.19)

From his perch on the wall, Diego watched the northern steam of his breath as it billowed up toward the stars. He thanked God for the millionth time that the wall stood there, keeping them on the other side—the monsters, the zombies, whatever you wanted to call them.

Amid the hordes, Diego noticed what used to be a young girl standing motionless, staring dead pan at him as the others swarmed around her. He couldn't

imagine how long it existed; there hadn't been known new life in over a decade.

#19 – Full Shame Shane (1.25.19)

Full of shame, Shane walked through the twilight of his suburban bubble, leafless trees opening up above him like palms cradling the blood moon glaring down at him.

You never know what people are doing when they're not being watched, Shane learned today, the most important lesson in his six young years.

Shane's feet crunched and scraped on the asphalt, as though drunk in confusion. He tried not to think of his grandfather.

The things we do when no one's watching.

#20 – Truss of Trees (1.25.19)

The frame of the structure was crafted with gold-plated alloy, but the bamboo canopy gave the impression that there was nothing remarkable about the small hut among the tight truss of trees.

However, Juan was strapped to an old wartime cot directly beneath the point where the rescue helicopter hovered, slowly combing the area to find his very person.

The gag muffled his voice and his eyes screamed in its stead, pleading to be heard through the awful obstruction of his tears.

#21 – Pink as the Water (1.25.19)

Leonard couldn't keep the grin off his face, an innocent display of glee that stood in stark contrast with its source. With each twirl of the mop on the floor this smile seemed to grow.

He remembered all that blood from the night before, the way the swirls of pink followed the mop across the floor.

There was nothing you couldn't clean. He thought fondly of his life, the cumulative tasks comprising his "career".

He pushed the mop for his Monday night client, a diaper factory.

Maybe later tonight he would make another mess.

#22 – Broken Teeth (1.26.19)

Curtis's henchmen held Stanley to the ground in a stranglehold as Curtis puffed on his cigar, probably seeming to loom at a great height from where Stanley lay.

"I don't know what to do with you, Stan," Curtis said, rotating his cigar between his thumb and pointer finger. "Every time I think I can trust you something like this happens."

Stanley tried to speak, but instead expunged a glob of blood, which seeped through his broken teeth.

"I loved you like a brother, Stanley."

#23 – Drunk on Adrenaline (1.26.19)

Drunk on adrenaline, vengeance, and testosterone, Powell tore through the ground with his shovel. He had finally managed to slaughter all his rivals, and was now determined to bury each body in its own plot out of tribute to his hatred for them rather than dump them in a mass grave.

Each of the thirteen cadavers had been acquired over many years. He stowed them in the bomb shelter of his remote mountain bunker, each of the repugnant faces degraded to varying degrees of rot.

Dawn waged its war on the stars, but Powell would not stop until he finished; he owed that much to himself.

#24 – The False Genius of His Craft (1.26.19)

Bronson spent his days crumbled into any given piece of furniture scattered around his penthouse, shielded from daylight by the heavy violet curtains hanging from windows reaching from floor to ceiling. He was once a famous artist. Well, he was still famous, but no longer an artist. At present he almost regretted his entire career, for the celebration he had received while he himself still believed in the false genius of his craft. He couldn't even remember when he learned the truth, but it never released him from its grasp.

#25 – This Obese Population (1.26.19)

Kenla switched the compressor hose to the next tire in a never-ending line. She was the most fit of all the camp's residents, and could not see the logic in leadership's decision to assign her to the auto garage post, which descended into sub-freezing temperatures, when the camp contained many more sensible prospects with all the fat women. There was not enough spare clothing available to offer the sort of natural insulation this population was born with. Objection proved futile. So she carried on with the tires, twelve hours at a clip.

#26 – A Slow Boil (1.26.19)

Every time Jesabelle danced on stage she imagined new means of escaping Davison, who was probably off testing new talent in each city they visited as she forced herself through each set.

The patrons of the clubs could detect nothing awry, of course, for Jesabelle threw her all into her performances.

Sometimes servitude blossoms like a slow boil, occurring unbeknownst to the subject.

Jesabelle danced and the crowd roared.

She saw Davison enter the room, zipping his fly.

#27 – Laboratory Hands (1.27.19)

Paxton placed the food plate on the shelf and spun the glass shield so that Sherman could take it.

The young man walked over and inhaled his chicken, mashed potatoes, and cranberry with his fingers.

He had never been spoken to, had never interacted with anyone aside from laboratory hands.

He and his twin brother had been split at birth, and had been nurtured in totally different worlds.

Simon, Sherman's twin, was set to win the Nobel Prize the next week.

#28 – Blood Sport (1.27.19)

Harleque stood in the center of the ring, the area the group used for both sermons and fights, ideological development and physical release.

Today, after Harleque delivered his address, they would witness a match that would determine the faction's deputy of defense.

The gathered crowd roared in support for the speaker's socialist message, driving up the pulse that would see the blood sport commence.

#29 – Return to Dust (1.27.19)

Belle couldn't force a sense of cordiality, but her beauty

afforded her many takers in trying to talk to her, shielding any opportunity for Eric to approach her.

So he watched from a distance, locked in a naked stare. Belle followed his whereabouts at all moments, but made sure not to make eye contact.

The prolonged distraction would not barre inevitability, however, and they both knew that in the end all would return to dust and she would fall into his hands.

#30 – Cowardly Comrade (1.27.19)

The mob had been staked outside Krueger's home for days since the trial commenced, which would carry beyond the foreseeable future.

Cramped beneath his desk, he almost laughed to think he once considered himself thick-skinned, prepared to face any obstacle that presented itself.

How wrong he was, how quickly such confidence, the cowardly comrade, will retreat.

He could cry and hide all he wanted at night, weather the death threats and pretend to serve on the side of justice.

In the end he would appear in court, ice cold.

#31 – Pack Your Bags (1.27.19)

"He has to go, Dan," Jenny said.

"Babe, he's my brother. Can't you please let it go?"

"Dan—he was sniffing my panties and jerking off in our bedroom. You're okay with that?"

"I didn't say that, Jesus. But what do you want me to do about it? He's my brother, he's been struggling with issues for years now."

"I hadn't noticed. Listen, Dan. Either I'm leaving or you need to get rid of him."

"Okay. I'll help you pack your bags."

#32 – Shadow of a Theory (2.27.19)

Lumberg mowed lawns with surgical precision and industrial determination. It was understood that he manicured over a hundred lawns of various acreage. His competition regarded him with contempt, believing that his illustrious work ethic was due to a compulsion to hide some dark secret. No details of such a secret ever emerged, not even the shadow of a theory, but people pushed such notions as gospel, however foggy the prospects of their veracity.

That didn't prevent the legend from mowing on.

#33 – Offed (1.27.19)

To be baby Phillip's plaything stood among the most dreaded of appointments in the kingdom.

There was no logic to Phillip's methods; they were impulses reacting to impulses.

He could point at you and a guard would cut your head off, often due to misinterpretations of Phillip's toddler gestures, which yielded in the murder of said guard for the offense of sabotage once the mistake had been recognized.

Phillip would touch his throat to signal for a drink— the plaything's throat would be slit, another act of sabotage resulting in the offing of another guard.

Often every guard and plaything would be offed, and Phillip would not receive his drink.

#34 – IV Drip (1.27.19)

Rump began her indiscretions with subtle insinuations directed at her bodyguards in retaliation for Giuardo's marital absence.

These insinuations eventually developed into acts of compulsive debaucheries. She sucked them off in the backseat of her transport vehicle, forced them to perform oral on her while she spoke to Giuardo on the phone.

Eventually she took to getting them to fuck her,

which secured a habit that evolved into an addiction which matured into a requirement like an IV drip.

#35 – Human Firewood (1.27.19)

Gonzo stared at the massive pyre, its flames reaching twenty feet high, with a curious lack of reaction for a boy who'd just set everyone he'd ever known ablaze in a summary incineration.

Black smoke wafted, carrying the stench of burning flesh, human firewood, a scene for which the screaming lumber provided a soundtrack.

Why he would do such a thing—not four months had passed since his thirteenth birthday—eluded him; he looked preposterous standing alone atop a hill beyond the city's gate as he watched his civilization burn.

#36 – Nervous Beams (1.27.19)

A dozen eyes peered through the same slat, illuminated by the spotlights pouring from the encirclement.

Several armed agents led the raid, the flashlights secured to their rifles casting nervous beams across the cellar.

"We've got something," announced the first man who entered.

Then a man, presumably the mission leader, made his way down the concrete steps, his form obscured by the haze of smoke and light.

He noticed the captives right away. "Bolt cutters."

#37 – Linguistic Failings (1.26.19)

Seger, prone to buckling under pressure, struggled to write what the hangmen wanted, but with each finger they cut off, a blinding pain that compounded his linguistic failings, blacking the world out beyond his own incoherent screaming, he regressed further into uselessness

"I can't do this," he screamed, or at least he thought that's what came out of his mouth.

He could comprehend their shouted responses just as unclearly as his own attempt to express himself.

"You will obey," the ring leader screamed. "Or more fingers!"

#38 – Retreating to the Kitchen (1.27.19)

Devony sat at the dining room table, struggling not to react to what she had seen of Barbara earlier that afternoon, when she discovered the unveiled beast lurking beneath her pretty skin.

The other attendees at the table, laughing jovially, betrayed no hint of awareness to this secret, even as the threat loomed near.

Barbara walked in with a tray of lasagna. She smiled at Devony. "Is everything okay, dear?"

"Yes, of course." Devony returned the smile, even as her soul froze over.

"Great," Barbara said, then retreated to the kitchen.

#39 – Double D. Sandy (1.28.19)

They called her Double D. Sandy. Not just to put her ample bust on blast, but because she needed one dick in her ass and the next in her sass or she couldn't be happy.

But her temperament and appetite for mammal connection did not equate, as she had the spirit of a third wave feminist and the carnal availability of a Thai comfort girl.

This enigma unsolved, she carried on with her crusade, breaking spirits as she rode chode, rod, and branch, never quite satiated, certainly never satisfied.

#40 – Martial Training (1.28.19)

Nikolas clamped his eyes tight till tears welled behind the lids, feeling the steel of his own gun turned on him, pressed into his neck.

The operation should have been a summer breeze, not unlike what could be found on the tropical island to which his crew planned to emigrate after this final heist.

They were well aware of security detail and the general clientele that utilized the bank's services; no one should have possessed martial training, especially at a branch so far off the grid.

That the soft elderly lady, who stopped by every Tuesday to deposit her social security check, provided justice before the cops could arrive, floored him.

#41 – How We Get What We Want (1.28.19)

Bubba pulled the toolbox from the back of his truck and made his way toward his sister's house.

He grumbled when he saw that the porch door was cracked open.

He walked inside. "Marsha?"

There came no response, so he followed the light escaping from the basement.

"Oh, God," he shouted when he reached the bottom of the stairs.

There Marsha lay, face-down in a pool of her own dark blood. Her head had been bashed in, and a knife was lodged up her shoulder blade.

We can't control how we get what we want.

#42 – Mass and Sky (1.28.19)

Syvyl's silhouette walked toward the horizon, a two-dimensional world of red and black, mass and sky. She still clutched the shears she had used to torture and bleed out those who had captured and killed Josalie.

Syvyl took no pride in the grisly deed, but what could she do? From childhood into multiple survival groups, several of which they wound up the only survivors, Josalie was all she had.

Then these pissants came upon them while they were sleeping.

In the end, she had to cut her losses.

#43 – The Edge of the Property (1.28.19)

Dilbert went at it hard as he watched Peggie Sue and Ambert Atton getting it on through the window. He was almost there when he heard footsteps on the wet grass.

"Huh?" Dilbert turned as Peggie Sue's father came closer. He stood and zipped up as he ran away.

"I'll get you, you little bastard!" hissed Peggie Sue's father.

Dilbert hid behind a tree at the edge of the property and watched Peggie Sue's father step up to the window.

Dilbert squinted and realized Peggie Sue's father was unzipping his pants.

#44 – This Profane Reign (1.28.19)

Muzza struggled with the cross on his back, a wall of hands reaching out to him as the entourage of guards held the crowd at bay.

Muzza saw nothing; not only did his blood drip into his eyes, but the light at the end of the tunnel of bodies shone blindingly.

"Make way, make way!" shouted one of the guards.

Muzza stumbled but regained balance without the need of his escort's assistance.

Soon blood would rain on this profane reign.

#45 – Plan F. (1.28.19)

Germaine sat in the stool as The Barber worked his magic on his black crop, almost blue amid the flashing steel of the legendary scissors.

Germaine had explained everything to The Barber, who, aside from the occasional reactionary grunt, maintained a stolid silence.

Germaine considered prompting further conversation, but did not want to offend the elder; it was known that The Barber maintained only the most well-paced and mannered conversations.

Finally, he said, "Defer to Plan F."

#46 – Creative Amid All This Hysteria (1.28.19)

"Leave me alone, woman!"

Delaney paced in his office for the past fifteen minutes, surveying his latest notes as his wife, Maura, followed him around like a stubborn shadow.

"Please, Delaney, stop for a moment! The children are starving! Soon we will be evicted."

"Rubbish!" Delaney roared. "Now leave me be! How can one be creative amid all this hysteria?"

"Your creativity is no longer of any consequence—you need to get a new job!"

"This is my work and if you don't leave my office I'll work you!"

#47 – Forgotten to the Gala (1.28.19)

To the guests gathered around where he lay in the fetal position on the bear rug, frothing at the mouth, it may have appeared that Dovermann, one of the nominees for Best Actor that year, was having a seizure.

In reality, coming from a space of green all but forgotten to the gala of industry elites in attendance, Dovermann could not live with knowing what he had learned about his contemporaries over the past two years.

Wayne Weiszel, an executive producer, stepped forward, withdrew a pistol, and put a bullet into Dovermann's brain, muttering, "He'd never last."

#48 – A Dozen Tiny Knives (1.29.19)

Faltooth's body was drenched in sweat, yet his throat was so dry it felt like a dozen tiny knives scraped his wind pipe every time he breathed.

He had traversed all the ecosystems of his land, and presently stumbled through the desert where rock structures began to appear, dotting the way toward the mountains of the north.

He dropped behind the shade of such a structure to

rest. He took out his small pouch of memories, opened it, and looked for the tooth.

Against what he lost, he gained all.

#49 – Familiar Mast (1.29.19)

Coilina sat on the beach, watching the sand cupped in her palm blow away with the wind.

She sensed that the rescue team had been compromised. Though immediate communication had been severed long ago, punctuality stood as a central virtue to the corps.

So she sat watching the breakers lash out and recede into the tide.

The pickup should have arrived at noon, give or take a few hours. It had already been two days.

Then she saw the familiar mast.

#50 – Off the Record (1.29.19)

Jules railed the line Chino had prepared for her and threw her head back as her body embraced the hit.

She fell back into the couch, crossed her legs, and straightened her skirt. "So, have I earned your trust?"

Chino broke another line and railed it with the cut plastic straw. "Not sure yet," he said, sniffing to clean his nose. "But at least we can talk."

"That's a good start," Jules said, pulling out a pen and notepad.

He touched her knee. "Off the record."

#51 – The Score (1.29.19)

The score had taken him two years, three months, four days, five hours, and six minutes to complete, yet after seven seconds of deliberation he pulled the trigger and sprayed his brains on the gold wallpaper.

The score would eventually rise to prominence as his post-humous magnum opus, but he could not both release it to the masses and continue to live at the same time.

No one arrived to carry the mantle and another great light went out with no replacement, dramatized by the fallen composer's most famous ballad of lament.

#52 – Artless Guilt (1.30.19)

Miguel had long been corporate's favorite custodian, a man who kept his head down and the floors shiny. If reason for corporate alarm arose, he would be made aware and dutifully follow the instructions of his superiors.

But such situations rarely arose, and he went about his tasks as passively as the air conditioner's hum, specially assigned to the night shift, when his unbiased services were most likely required.

He would clean the lobby and main corridors until summoned to whatever hiccup awaited him.

The execs would lead the way and leave him a handsome tip before disappearing into their immunity.

#53 – Stepped out of Her Skin (1.30.19)

Some people own wig collections, some collections of faces. Lola belonged to the second category.

She had been born with a face, yes, but had lived so many other lives since the first time she stepped out of her skin, how could she explain that she was an actress of humanity, had stepped into the skin of others, had borne every shade of experience?

Though born with one, she had lost track of her first face, and she was now a void of nothingness beneath.

#54 – Awaiting Her Arrival in Terror (1.30.19)

Anviel spread her wings and jumped off the tower. She glided over the hillside toward the village, which had been awaiting her arrival in terror for several weeks now.

Though there had been claims of a return countless times over the decades, all the peoples of the land knew that the situation had shifted in recent years, that the disconnect between the rulers and the peasantry had grown too vast and too imposing to ignore.

The village came into Anviel's view and she hovered above the square, finding it vacant, doors and windows shuttered.

#55 – Just One Tipoff (1.30.19)

Coach Reinman had received a warning phone call several days earlier, but made no moves to run or go into hiding. He would face the music directly.

Dozens of students over the past three decades, most of them budding young women, and the thought of getting caught never held any weight in his mind.

Just one tipoff, and he knew it was all over. So he waited for the authorities, not even seeking refuge in the bottle.

Then the door slammed in and he blinked.

#56 – Crumbling Further Each Day (1.30.19)

Ringha held her children close as they hid behind a fallen rafter in the back of the decrepit warehouse, its foundation crumbling further each day.

Tears of fear fell down her daughter's cheek and her son stared ahead in defiance, prepared for any outcome— nothing could be worse than what they had already endured.

"Clear!" they heard a voice call from across the space.

Ringha closed her eyes in relief, but it would be hours before they moved on.

#57 – Bullseye in an Open Field (1.31.19)

The customer standing before Brett drove his nerves to the edge of the distress he had worked so hard to keep neutral over the past few months he had been employed at Darling's Cupcake Shoppe and Bakery, dressed in his pink apron like a bullseye in an open field.

"Why are there no sprinkle hearts on the Valentine's Day donuts?"

"Sir," Brett said, steam now spewing from his ears, "the donuts are baked in the shape of hearts."

"Where is the continuity—give me your corporate number."

"Get it yourself, I quit."

#58 – Incinerate Them! (1.31.19)

Dunga surveyed the area as the tank made its way slowly but surely through the rocky terrain, small brush providing its only vegetation. Arms resting on the sides of the open top door, she depended on the binoculars in her hands to tell her the truth; this was hostile territory, and sovereignty hadn't been established in many years.

"Can't see anything," she said to her crew below. "Keep going nice and slow; we're bound to come across someone."

Just then a bullet buzzed by her head.

She dropped down.

"Incinerate them!"

#59 – The Unseen Figure (1.31.19)

Marsha stopped walking once she determined that the footsteps behind were following her. "Did Gershon send you?" she asked, her voice barely above a whisper.

The footsteps walked closer, and she dared not turn around. Then the unseen figure stood directly behind her; she could hear it breathing.

She forced the slowing of her own breathing, but the pressure of her nerves climbed ever-further.

It seemed that the other did not intend to speak as the seconds passed.

Then it was gone and she could breathe again.

#60 – The Anti-Preventative Law (1.31.19)

Doctor Verhindern threw the last stack of folders into his

massive furnace, folding his hands behind his back as he watched the records of twenty-five years of work burn to flaky ash.

With the passing of the new anti-preventative law, he couldn't afford to leave one trace of evidence illustrating his life's legacy. He never harbored anything but the view that he had operated toward the benefit of humanity at large.

He was the aborter of nightmare and obligation.

Now they would abort him, if able.

#61 – All Manner of Mischief (1.31.19)

News had circulated among the townspeople that the occupying soldiers had been sowing all manner of mischief since their arrival, even murder.

But Nora Sanger didn't mind, she liked the men lodging at her house. Toby, her husband, was an enlisted man, and she had always deemed him a coward and didn't expect him to return.

She was a beautiful woman, this Nora Sanger, and had not felt a man's touch in some time. She had heard many tales of rape, but her men barely looked at her; it all almost made her feel jealous.

#62 – Two Inches from the Stud (1.31.19)

"I told you to get close to him, not fuck him, you dumb bitch!"

"What was I supposed to do? I did it for us—he was losing interest in me."

Brandon punched the wall, breaking through sheet rock, barely two inches from the stud. "So now what? You've got the guy wrapped around your finger?"

"I didn't say that. But now at least we have time to consider our options."

Brandon snorted. "And what are our options—what are you worth now? You're like a lame race horse."

#63 – Unique Emotional Markers (1.31.19)

Durnst read through the reports stacked on his desk with rapt attention yet mechanical speed. More of the same for the most part. Most of the subjects existed in identical patterns with the exception of their unique emotional markers. He was on the hunt for abnormalities, behaviors that stood in steep contrast to the status quo.

Durnst scanned through at least one hundred such files a day. Even if he never found was he was looking for, the administration considered his among the most virtuous of work.

#64 – Stretches Spent in the Slammer (1.31.19)

Reggie had been promoted to contraband distributor after three weeks in the prison.

He had just gotten through five years of civilian life after many stretches spent in the slammer.

He held many jobs during his various sentences, but never had experience working behind the scenes, without administrative protection.

Every Tuesday he would make his rounds, passing out gifts and purchases between prisoners.

On this Tuesday he forced himself to DeGray's cell, sensing with every delivery that the murderer wanted to kill him more and more.

#65 – Impending Defeat (2.1.19)

Glenda Marceles, the Democratic presidential nominee, glared at the monitors throughout the office. Staffers and party members shuffled around, trying to make sense of the impending defeat.

"Why did you make me do it?" she hissed at her manager, Ellis Wentz, in reference to the latest scandal to guild her legacy.

Ellis smiled. "Glenda, don't turn this on me. You knew the risks. I told you."

Glenda's face reddened. "You know what, Ellis? Maybe

one of us won't survive tonight."

#66 – Factions Swarmed the Streets (2.1.19)

It began with the music, primal expressions of rebellion. As time went on and the scene's membership fermented, the clan flexed, fomenting at the edge of plan and execution. The injustices of the world had driven them into a frenzy. They released this frenzy at their shows, which to many attendees presented a religious experience. Then the venues turned them away, banishing the worshipped tones. There were more adherents than the system had anticipated, however, and factions soon swarmed the streets.

#67 – Shallow Waters (2.1.19)

Juniper waded in the shallow waters, her nude form slowly maneuvering through the marshy grasses. She seemed focused on a plane removed from the serenity that

surrounded her, perhaps even more serene.

With her back to the shore, she watched the sunset's rippled rays bounce on the water's edge.

She turned around and saw him standing there, her shock allowing a mere gasp. He stared down with his dark black eyes, the accusation blaring clear.

"You've finally come for me."

#68 – Dwarf from the Southern Steppe (2.1.19)

Edwin walked in, resembling a dwarf from the southern steppe. He snorted deep and swallowed his phlegm. He walked past the gathered workers, readying themselves to set on their routes.

Then he stepped up to the doorway of the manager's office. "Hey, numb nuts. Did you see what happened with Marceles?"

Snyder, the manager, shook his head, as if able to ward off his frustration with such a gesture. "Don't start with this shit, Edwin."

"Sore losers. You can dish it out, but you can never take it."

#69 – White Wedding Gone Red (2.1.19)

One minute it was a wedding like any other, the next it was a scene of pure pandemonium.

Just after the cutting of the cake came the cutting of the guests by the guests themselves, and how their blood, the sight alone, made them crave even more of it, the plasma inside the plasma.

The bride screamed in a soul-tearing pitch, which drove the guests even further into their insanity, their possessed carnage.

White wedding gone red.

#70 – In the Gardens Below (2.2.19)

Candace, unnoticed where she stood on the balcony, a dainty figure dressed in white, watched her father and their longtime maid, Cheyenne, laughing in the gardens below.

Every time Candace's father, Bernard, made Cheyenne laugh, the woman would touch his arm.

Since her mother had disappeared—by death, leaving the nest, no one could be sure—, she had been suspicious of all women not biologically part of the family.

She trained her eyes on Cheyenne's neck, the woman who used to sew her mother's dresses, and imagined it snapping.

#71 – Complimentary Coffee (2.2.19)

Cyber sat at the counter, seething. If he wanted to wait an extra twenty minutes for his food he wouldn't have called for takeout. He sipped his complimentary coffee, forty minutes since he called lazed on the couch.

He didn't feel like looking around, so he stuffed the spent sugar packets into a small plastic creamer cup.

Jesus, how long did it take to make two sandwiches?

Then the door slammed open and an armed assailant entered. "Everyone on the ground!"

#72 – An Army of Cops, Feds, and Press (2.2.19)

Caesar hustled to pack the bags his cousin had entrusted to him, having not investigated their contents as he promised, carrying two at a time up the concrete stairs into the loading dock, where he tossed them into the back seat of his antiquated Jeep. This is all he had to do to earn his freedom, his cousin told him. Transport the six bags on this date without tampering with them. Once loaded, he pulled out of the garage and was greeted by an army of cops, feds, and press, helicopters circling in the smoggy sky above.

#73 – An Added Friction Entered His World (2.2.19)

Winston didn't know whether or not to feel guilty for signing off on the Langston account, but from

the moment his pen left the paper, he knew he'd entered a different realm of power. The very air around him assumed a new pressure, an added friction entered his world.

"Thank you, sir," said Robert Langston himself, who had attended the signing ceremony.

Winston swallowed and nodded, suddenly feeling an overwhelming emptiness.

"No turning back now."

#74 – Your Role as My Servant (2.2.19)

Bantam sat across the table from Nebraska, Hoodsey's widow. He had chosen a sleepy cafe in the center of the village for their rendezvous. A warm breeze passed through the establishment, all of its windows bared open to disperse the heat weltering within.

When Bantam finished relaying his perspective on how to proceed with the mechanisms Hoodsey had initiated in life, Nebraska leaned in and said, "You must take me for a fool. If you didn't, you would recognize your role as my servant."

#75 – Lush in the Air (2.3.19)

Budsy climbed out of Slim's pickup truck at the bait shop. Breathing in the pine in the air that he had grown to consider a part of himself since he'd began his weekend forays into the locale over two decades ago, he followed Slim, a native to the sticks town, up the creaky steps and into the shop, dust floating lush in the air.

The register man looked up, grimacing when he saw Budsy. "What the hell do you want?" he said, throwing down the tractor magazine.

#76 – Before Bureaucracy Caught Up (2.3.19)

They'd sent Brunson into the sewers recently, but he'd already exiled himself long ago; it was only a matter of time before bureaucracy caught up to him.

He didn't quite enjoy his subterranean existence, but it gave him time to think about the path that had led him there.

That was why he was down below: the path, not his own decisions. The world order did not reflect nature, and all the remaining men and women fell subject to this global perversion.

#77 – The Perfect Question Mark (2.3.19)

Every set of eyes in the room was locked on Shannon's body, the perfect question mark of flesh, leaning on the counter.

The associate's glasses reflected a bubble of gum popping on her pink lips as he tried to maintain conversation, the verbal representative of all men present, their interest much to the chagrin of their women.

While the other mammals struggled with their impulses, Rogan spotted what he and Shannon came for and left with it undetected.

#78 – He Continued (2.4.19)

Jeremiah stepped light on his toes through the forest, cautious not to make a sound so close to the enemy base.

Crickets and birds filled the silence as he made his way along, nervously looking this way and that.

Then he came upon an unmanned clearing, where five mounds of recently backfilled dirt were arranged in a row.

Five of the six missing.

Who and where was the sixth?

A cold sweat dawned on his face.

He continued.

#79 – Polka Dot Abundance (2.4.19)

Everything having to do with Mary Lou came down to polka dots, whatever the colors happened to be. Cute polka dot dresses for her lush polka dot figure; polka dot bubblegum and polka dot blowjobs, in polka dot abundance.

One day a blotch of red ink fell from the sky, a massive sphere of liquid that fell like a planet from the heavens, first collapsing upon itself and then enveloping everything in proximity.

Mary Lou screamed through the spray of her bloodied polka dot existence.

#80 – Into Pulp (2.4.19)

The clinic strapped Travis into his chair and played reel after reel of material that he could not remember, could not even comprehend if he did. With eyes glazed over, his mind melted into pulp, to be restructured in their image, he stared into the screen, the single point of his vision drinking the colorful images at the periphery.

He would no longer be himself once the program came to its scheduled conclusion.

Friends and family would recognize him by face, but he was no longer he.

#81 – Modern Grand Theft Auto (2.4.19)

The cars all screeched into the parking lot at the precisely scheduled moment, and a ball of light appeared in the center of where they would all collide had the ball not expanded and become a portal that transported them into another city, where the cars all screeched out into another garage in different directions, different fates for these glistening objects of modern grand theft auto in an era of bright lights and black holes, of being anywhere else you wanted to be on a whim.

#82 – Flirting with Intimacy (2.4.19)

Dmitri and Kathleen began hating each other a mere six months into their excursion, a recon mission to discover what happened to the arctic team, who had gone missing the previous year.

They worked well enough together before they made the mistake of flirting with intimacy, allowing passions to corrupt the clarity of their investigation.

So they broke the territory up between themselves to investigate independently rather than as a pair, as had been agreed since the earliest planning phases.

#83 – He Kept Their Hope Alive (2.4.19)

Professor Brigert had a reputation as a shadowy tight ass, but his students revered him if not only for his direct acquaintances with progressive policy makers and cultural dignitaries.

The students viewed him as the great liaison between these dignitaries and their political opinions— they naively believed that they could inspire him through their conviction, that they could influence his views.

He was well aware of this, of course, and he kept their hope alive.

#84 – The Coup Orchestrators Descended (2.4.19)

Only God knows how many people were required to carry out the operation, but they did.

Using only radios, they tracked Senator Bream from the capitol building to a remote cabin in Arkansas, where she met with Representative Schlit and Justice Mariner.

Fate crushed the false sense of security felt among the trio when the coup orchestrators came down like a lightning strike upon the rendezvous.

#85 – Dipper Rapidly Chipped a Niche (2.5.19)

As the Grounds Manager of the Buck Wild Country Club, Dipper rapidly chipped a niche for himself as an individual who, at a price, could contain what happened on the grounds, keep the unseemly out of sight and out of mind.

He became a dealer of secrets, a dark human rolodex of the club's clientele.

People went missing, wives and children, but no one asked questions; wallets got thicker and Dipper's contact list expanded.

#86 – She Who Aloofly Approached (2.5.19)

Marley sat with auto part crew every morning, a group of young men who met on the side stoop of the auto part store, despite having no affiliation with the business.

"Yaw Boomer," said Klaus, a fat one in his early twenties who always gave the impression that he was half asleep. "Check out what's comin' our way."

Boomer and the other three heads among them turned toward she who aloofly approached, all of them gawking.

#87 – Twenty-Four Hours with the Cadaver (2.5.19)

Maria would spend twenty-four hours with the cadaver

and know enough about the subject to create a perfect likeness of the departed in human clay.

She would then burn the cadaver upon a cross amid a massive blaze and the new being would open its eyes, a non-being determined to fulfill every expectation of the left-behind, never to receive more than disappointment once installed in its old life.

#88 – Millions upon Millions (2.5.19)

Versick had been Senator Cameron's bodyguard for three years, was privy to much of the information millions upon millions of Americans and people around the world would do anything to possess. He stood in meetings, guarded the door from outside, was never once questioned by Cameron in regards to his loyalty. But no one can really know who they should trust. Though one may take an oath to take a bullet for you, they are not exonerated from the possibility of weaponizing the truth.

#89 – Bar Crawl (2.5.19)

Nathan noticed that the stranger had been following his group's bar crawl through the city shortly after midnight.

As in a movie, all he could see was the bottom half of the lanky man's face under the hood of his sweatshirt.

Nathan decided to act as though nothing was out of tune, smiling and laughing with his friends, who were completely oblivious to their specter.

Eventually he excused himself to the bathroom.

As he peed, he heard a voice: "We haven't forgotten you."

#90 – National Organ Farm (2.6.19)

Roulta ran down the aisles of the national organ farm, stowing choice selections into the cooler she rolled behind her, and bolted from the refrigerator once she finished.

After months of preparation, her faction's

tech team had managed to crack the farm's security system for seven minutes, during which time her handlers were able to block off all access to her escape route.

The group she belonged to was strapped for personnel, so she was sent on the mission by herself, protected by what base claimed to be absolute security. Until she saw him at the final door.

"So fast. Perhaps you forgot something?"

#91 – Easy Pill to Swallow (2.6.19)

Leone worked at the office for around three weeks before Loretta began digging her claws into him.

It started innocently enough, just checking in on him here and there, making sure he was fitting in.

They were both single so he had no reason not to reciprocate and see where things would go. Besides, Loretta's beauty was revered, which made spending time

with her an easy pill to swallow.

When they became intimate everything changed.

Bars descended from the sky, keeping him in place.

Soon all breathable air would disappear from his world.

#92 – Berkin's Office (2.7.19)

Tom followed Sergio down the hall as soon as he left Berkin's office, knowing that Sergio wouldn't know how to handle himself after the meeting—he said so that morning, just before he stepped in to face the music.

"Serg, wait up."

Sergio rounded the corner and Tom found him leaning against the wall. "I need to get the fuck out of this place."

"Yeah," Tom said, preparing to issue some encouraging verbiage.

"But first I will see that communist piece of shit die, even if I have to burn with him."

#93 – The Grinder that Produced Their Funds (2.7.19)

Every morning, even though all the other workers drove their own vehicles to the shop, Bench stood across the parking lot from where Roger parked, chain smoking cigarettes, leaning against the painted block exterior of the grinder that produced their funds, as they all waited for the manager, Duncan, the only one entrusted with keys, even though he was typically the last to arrive.

Roger would catch Bench staring at him from time to time, but he was finished extending cordiality; Bench had already shown his true colors.

#94 – Heavily Shielded by Pedestrian Traffic (2.7.19)

Having already been dressed for over an hour, Marcia waited a moment to pull off the covers, jump off the couch (the only suitable place where she could sleep in the apartment), and follow her father down the sidewalk, heavily shielded by pedestrian traffic.

She squinted with angry contemplation as her father walked up to a house and knocked, to be greeted by a pretty yet tired-looking woman dressed in a dirty gown.

The woman kissed both of his cheeks and let him in.

Marcia waited until the door closed before walking toward the front porch.

#95 – Comfortable as an Antagonist (2.8.19)

Marfisboro felt that Transon had been needling him since the day the other man appeared on the scene at the factory. Most in his acquaintance could consider Marfisboro a fair, level man, courteous even, despite his own rough edges, but such a reception did not represent Transon's impression of the man.

The space between them closed in as Transon became more comfortable as an antagonist.

One day a group of Marfisboro's allies converged

upon Transon (without Morfisboro's knowledge) and showed him what was what.

#96 – To Distribute His Roses (2.8.19)

Kelly looked over the other nine girls as they all waited for Sean to distribute his roses, displaying her best smile while exerting all her will to prevent herself from killing her competition right then and there.

He'd already given roses to Michelle, Donna, and Hillary, all selections she deemed inferior to what she could bring to the table.

"Kelly," he said, smiling with a charm that disarmed the blood-storm raging in her veins.

#97 – From Beneath the Earth's Crust (2.8.19)

Wissen walked among the relics, artifacts mined from beneath the earth's crust indicative of a former reign of human prosperity yet providing no correlation between the forgotten society

and any peoples populating the planet today, and reflected on the frailty of the human condition, how quickly what we deem eternal can be swiped from the terrain of man without a second thought by divinity, who could both create life and just as easily take it away.

#98 – Civilization Had Pulsed Within (2.8.19)

"There she blows, eh, Lenny?"

"Aye, captain."

The men stared at their newly discovered island, a black mass burnt into a pink and orange sunset; civilization had pulsed within the island's overgrowth for hundreds of years, but that meant nothing to the new arrivals, men of the sea with no particular loyalties to individual lands.

"The plunder that awaits."

Lenny looked askance at the captain; the man had carried through his end of the bargain, and, slipping his pistol from its holster, he would carry through with his.

#99 – Like Children Having a Tantrum (2.9.19

Ricardo hated being in the supermarket with his mother. She was a marginally attractive woman beneath her extra padding, but her breasts enjoyed the benefit, always pressed out against her blouses like children having a tantrum. He hated that she let them show, never made an effort to maintain a sense of decency. He hated being fourteen and knowing that his perfumed mother, always without a stable man in her life, viewed each day as a new advertisement campaign.

#100 – She Looked at Him with Disgust (2.9.19)

Jansen ran up with another box as his brother, Steven, ran down; Jansen had been helping Steven and his girlfriend, Beth, move into their new condo for the past two hours.

Jansen brought the box up to the bedroom, finding Beth sorting through the boxes the brothers already brought in.

"You can't run away from this forever," he told her.

She looked at him with disgust. "I don't understand why you don't mind your own damned business."

"He's my brother. It is my business."

#101 – To Insinuate a Possible Backhand (2.9.19)

"Don't you ever speak to your mother like that!" Fontaine screamed at Ponto.

The boy stared at his mom's beau, the man who seemed to have dropped from the sky like an emperor intent on claiming his throne. "You stay out of this, *forestero!*"

Fontaine stepped up to the boy, hand raised to insinuate a possible backhand.

"Fontaine, no!" Ponto's mother cried out.

Fontaine lowered his hand. "If you were my son, you'd be bleeding."

#102 – Promise to Keep its Existence a Secret (2.9.19)

Nine-years-old, innocent beneath his mischievous thirst for knowledge and experience, Holt giggled as he watched the images on the screen, a collage of innocuous yet obscene graphics that alternated like a strobe light. He had acquired the link after badgering a classmate whose brother had shown it to him; the brother, several years older, had made Holt's friend promise to keep its existence a secret. Holt's friend couldn't resist telling Holt about the content, not realizing how insistent Holt could be about getting what he wanted.

Holt got the link in the end, and now his remaining innocence would unravel.

#103 – A Blasphemously Unjust Ruling (2.10.19)

Katalon sat in a ball in the corner of his cell—an apartment, really—, as he had since he arrived at the Kendall-Parker lockup facility three and a half months earlier.

He refused to indulge in the accommodations his remorseful colleagues had set in place for him as reparations for what they deemed a blasphemously unjust ruling—which they still fought against with the force of their full power.

But Katalon was already a broken man before his incarceration began. He acted in good faith, but couldn't unsee the truth.

#104 – The Straight Apple (2.10.19)

"You can't expect me to say that shit on the air," said Morrison Sinclair, the host of primetime liberal talk show, The Straight Apple, as the commercial break ran its course.

"Morrison, we don't have a choice," countered program manager Kyle Montrose. "No one knows that Marceles knew a God damned thing about the raid. We need to buy time."

39

"Morrison, we—" one of the show's producers said into Morrison's earpiece.

Morrison cut the voice off. "Hold on. Listen, Kyle, my viewers trust me. We can't keep feeding them these lies."

"Morrison," the producer chimed in again, "we've been on the air."

#105 – Creamy Dark Chocolate Skin (2.10.19)

Kiki moved her body side to side to the rhythm of the music, expertly swaying her hips in front of her dance fitness class. She smiled widely as her students followed along, her teeth blinding white against her creamy dark chocolate skin, her mighty long hair swaying in its ponytail.

Kiki was a customer favorite and drew a loyal clientele to her classes.

She looked to the back of the studio and saw him standing there.

Some people liked her too much.

#106 – Black against a Universe of White (2.11.19)

Blanco started questioning whether he was truly alive or pushing through purgatory when he came upon the embassy, a hulking structure of stone standing black against a universe of white, a swirl of snow and wind.

Feeling detached from his body, he moved one foot after the other, each feeling like a cinder block millions of flesh miles away.

He'd run out of food long ago, and had since been eating snow. No one knew he was alive, and he wasn't sure if they would want him to be.

#107 – The Teleprompter-Driven Throne (2.11.19)

Melanie's makeup artist worked her magic on the late-night star, who, as she had every night before going live, reflected upon the career and life choices that led her to the teleprompter-driven throne.

The sex, drugs, and murder of which she covered at times made her feel culpable in the country's culture of crime.

But none of that mattered now; the modern span of human attention only lasted as long as the next news cycle. Why would anyone care about the twists of her ten-year career?

#108 – The Stranger (2.12.19)

"Get yo' hands off of me, boy," Tika protested, moving closer to her friend Wanda in their VIP booth.

"Come on, ma," the man said, slipping into the booth.

"Yo man, that as far as you gonna get," Tika promised.

"Hey brotha."

The stranger looked up and found a bouncer standing over him. "What's good, man, can't you see I'm busy?"

Tika implored the bouncer with a pleading eye.

The stranger touched her leg.

"Let's go, motherfucker," growled the bouncer.

#109 – She Pulled the Trigger as He Came (2.12.19)

Ronda rode Rod's rod with purpose, as if acquiring a blessing from the gods. "Yes!" she cried out, her spine curling as she rolled her body over him.

"Oh yeah, that's good, baby," Rod said, his legs spread wide in the bed, creating a tent under the sheets, Ronda's little body cradled tight over his groin, making him feel that she was sucking on him with each rise and fall.

Behind her back, Ronda readied her gun, the true purpose of this visit, and pulled the trigger as he came.

#110 – MF Childhood Services (2.12.19)

Jimmy noticed Mrs. Jensen since his first day of custodial employment at MF Childhood Services, an organization that facilitated pediatric observation for volunteer families.

The facility prided itself as an outlet for philanthropic

interests, championing a committed board of directors and amassing a large panel of donors. Along with this display of highbrow bureaucracy stood a strong sense of theological occultism.

Ever since that first day, he would find Mrs. Jansen smiling at him.

#111 – The Spine of Their Trade (2.12.19)

The new recruits all felt that there was no turning back now as they made their way along the side of Testa's building, backs pressed against the bricks.

Rotating spotlights scanned the property in a steady rhythm.

They had to take out Testa and all men they came across going in and coming out. There would be no investigating the background of their targets, no insight as to the nature of Testa's business in general.

This anonymity would be the spine of their trade, that which to keep them alive.

#112 – Muscle to Represent the Will of the People (2.12.19)

Bargmen winced as the nurse, who traveled with the campaign as a mobile medic to attend the congressman as he made his way along the campaign trail in hopes of arriving in the Oval Office, squeezed the contents of the syringe into his arm, transforming a mortal man into a "muscle to represent the will of the people," which just so happened to be his campaign slogan. Three weeks straight on the road while maintaining his current post with great attention. He needed a boost.

#113 – One of the Venue's Antiquities (2.13.19)

Thomas glanced at the marquee and stepped up to the outside ticket window. He paid and they handed him his paper ticket, which was one of the venue's antiquities that kept him coming back.

He came alone every Wednesday as a mid-week reward to himself. Cici could do whatever she wanted, he would have his solitary cinema time.

He bought a soda and popcorn and took a seat in the theater. He remained the only attendant as the curtains parted.

#114 – Being Valentine's Day (2.14.19)

Jeremiah's lower back ached by the fourth hour of his shift. He worked at a greeting card store. Being Valentine's Day, business was booming. Many lovers came and went; he wondered how many couples stole time to covertly buy each other cards at this very store. He had no one to buy a card for, no one to buy a card for him, no one to look forward to speaking to, even. Would he want such a person in his life?

A customer stepped up.

"Find everything you were looking for?"

"Yes, thank you."

#115 – Center of his Cell (2.16.19)

Elmore stared at the intercom button in the center of his cell or whatever it was that confined him; all he knew was he couldn't leave and he didn't know who held him.

The intercom button seemed to reflect the shining darkness of the space, the eternal nothingness.

He was only allowed to press the button once, a red half-sphere as if a crimson baseball were burrowed halfway into the table.

The emergency they alluded to arrived without warning.

His eyes burst like water balloons.

#116 – A Safe Space (2.16.19)

Jameson did his best not to interact with the clients, especially those who looked like Mrs. Killerston. But, as a ship hand, there were those times when the need for his services outshone his desire to maintain a safe space between himself and those he found desirable.

"Jameson," Mrs. Killerston said one afternoon when they were anchored in shallow waters just off the reef, "do you have any idea of when my husband will return?"

"No, madam, I do not."

#117 – Carrion (2.17.19)

Jenk sucked the meat from the bone, making sure not to waste anything. He had been forced to resort to vultures and at times what would be their carrion.

Desperation had driven him to the edge of the standards he had come to expect in his privileged life.

He ate his game with no pleasure of its taste.

Companionship had ceased long ago. He had lost interest in maintaining a civilized appearance.

There was no one to appear before.

#118 – Shadows of the Cave (2.17.19)

Peter sat crouched in the deepest shadows of the cave he claimed for hiding since the latest regiment crept through the forest, their singular mission being none other than to end the life of any human being they crossed.

His family had been taken care of during the last regional cleansing—a process that presented no clear criteria, as communications had largely broken down.

He did not even know the identities of those who carried out the missions, the men or women dressed in black tactical gear, opaque goggles, and oxygen masks.

#119 – Activities Coordinated of the Street (2.18.19)

"Who was that?" asked Boris as he returned to the bedroom, drying himself off with a burgundy towel.

"Oh, no one, my sweet," Vishna said, wrapped in the bedsheet like a cocoon.

Boris grunted. "Didn't sound like no one."

She smiled and he let it go; he couldn't get hung up on every distraction when his primary focus was to keep his street activities coordinated.

He dropped his towel and stood before her, rubbing his belly. "But, before I go..."

#120 – Hundreds of Industry Elites (2.19.19)

Clayton Harris did not process the announcement for nearly a minute, remaining seated with a distant stare as though encaged in the open. Hundreds of industry elites cheered his victory.

He had never considered acting before Van Mauersteen approached him with the role of the rogue blacksmith in his latest feature.

Clayton had been on the scene as the reporters conducted impromptu interviews with witnesses after the big accident, a

twenty-six-car pileup on I95. Mauersteen had seen the clip featuring Clayton, and knew Clayton had what he needed.

"You won," said Mauersteen, seated beside him.

#121 – Watch over the Crypt (2.19.19)

Kurt had the boys rotate their watch over the crypt in shifts—whoever had proven trustworthy to uphold the task. This custom had been maintained for years, as Kurt had developed somewhat of a following of devotees, but none had reason to believe his myths were real, that the crypt belonged to the spirit of a forgotten deity. The deity would remain in eternal slumber, yet he claimed countless legions were determined to discover the doorway of the gate they protected.

#122 – The One with the Most to Lose (2.19.19)

Lester could bring himself to say nothing if not what he

saw earlier in the storage shed, so he resolved to say nothing at all as he stared at his dinner plate, the others at the table speaking in jovial tones.

Janice, herself the one with the most to lose, stood as the most energized of all. She spared no concern of being called out. She locked eyes with Lester. "Is everything okay, Lester? You seem... absent."

#123 – The Moment He Abducted Her (2.19.19)

"Why don't you love me?" he screamed, bending down to hover over her cowering body where it lay, her arms bound behind her back, mouth gagged with a soiled rag.

She stared back with wide bloodshot eyes, utter confusion pouring with the tears; she had never seen this man before.

In the time between the moment he abducted her, with the aid of chloroform, and now, waking up to this barrage of threats, accusations, and demands, he

could have brought her anywhere.

#124 – Less-than-Couth Techniques (2.19.19)

They called him Howdy Doody; he didn't like it, but it stuck, and that's what they called him. Served him right, thought the community in unanimous silence, as Howdy Doody was in business uglier than his acquired name, how the mayor himself referred to him behind his back with contemptuous bite.

Howdy Doody ran the local watering hole, Shamrock Shack, and utilized less-than-couth techniques in his hiring practices.

#125 – The Devil She Didn't Know (2.19.19)

Being the dead of night, Kirsten couldn't see more than twenty yards ahead, moonlight glimmering on the rippling waters of the lake.

She turned back toward the house; he would be upon her any second now if she didn't put water and space between them, and fast.

She couldn't see him if he were an arm's length away, so she plunged into the lake; unable to see in either direction, she decided on the devil she didn't know.

Fear pushed her along.

He arrived at the water's edge and screamed.

#126 – The Benefit of Science (2.19.19)

Timmons struggled to hold his nerves at bay as he sat in the waiting room chair. He crossed one leg, then the other. He twiddled his thumbs, scanned through the magazines arranged on the table in front of him. He was too distracted to digest the words, and went back to looking around the office.

He was the only client present, if that's what one could call him. More of a subject than a patient, he had sacrificed the promise of good health for the benefit of science.

"Mr. Timmons, we're ready for you."

#127 – The Ice Clinked (2.19.19)

Dominic stood at the window and looked out at where Meredith and Ed stood just beside the fenced-in garden at the far corner of the lawn.

The sun's glare on the window's glass would have obscured Dominic's figure from where they stood if they suspected his distant gaze, but they were preoccupied with their own concerns.

Dominic moved the glass in his hand and the ice clinked. *What concerns could they share?* he asked himself as he took a swig from the whiskey, the hard, unbiased confidant when no one else remained.

#128 – Doppleganger (2.19.19)

Doreen Clemens, he moaned in his mind as she worked his dick with her mouth and hands much better than she used them to report the news and hold her microphone.

She had the desperation of a true professional,

however; otherwise, why would she agree to swallowing the full capacity of the seed he had built up in exchange for a real interview?

He moaned; she did excellent work, indeed.

Then the door opened.

"Doreen?" asked the doppleganger of the man she sucked, the intended subject of the meeting.

#129 – A Lanky Human Walking Stick (2.19.19)

Booboo the mime made his way down the street like a lanky human walking stick, contorting his body in ways the people he passed never imagined possible. They laughed nervously as he ambled past, his head seeming to spin on a spindle, a smile painted in white paint on an otherwise deadpan face. His eyes seemed to glow yet the irises were so dark that they appeared black, like coins of ink pressed into his lazy yellow eyes.

#130 – The Urban Darkness (2.19.19)

When the crew broke from their pre-mission huddle, synthesizing group solidarity by combining their collective lust for revenge, they jumped into the van and it sped toward Sanchez's base in the industrial sector of the city.

When they reached the destination neighborhood, they killed their headlights and coasted in the urban darkness.

A few lots from Sanchez's building a police cruiser turned its lights on.

"Fuck!" screamed the driver, just then seeing Sanchez exit his building.

#131 – Devout Devotee of the Movement (2.20.19)

Branson finally learned how to block out Ernst's voice after days of nonstop one-sided conversation.

Branson didn't choose Ernst as a scouting partner but knew that the younger man was a devout devotee of their movement.

"I should have baked more bread," Ernst said from behind the massive boulder whose shade they used for their mid-afternoon stop. "My mother says I bake the best bread she's ever tasted."

Branson grunted indifferently as he bit into a piece of cured jerky.

#132 – They Gasped in Unison (2.20.19)

Blood-eyed, screeching terror replaced the ideological awe of the crowd as a trio of masked men rushed the presenter from backstage, overtaking him from behind; the crowd knew it wasn't an act when they saw the curved blade pierce through the presenter's sternum, blood splaying at the feet of the front row attendees.

They didn't follow their spiritual leader for no reason, however, and couldn't bring themselves to flee. They would follow him into death if necessary.

Then he looked up with glowing eyes and they gasped in unison.

#133 – To or with Him (2.21.19)

Carrie sat alone at her assigned table. The other guests were busy tearing it up on the dance floor. When they returned, the seat to her right would remain vacant, as Ty had decided not to show up in the end. Being honest with herself, she scratched that last thought—she didn't have evidence to support the idea that he'd decided anything, he simply didn't show or call to follow up. Anything could have happened to or with him, and she made a decision of her own to believe that it was all another letdown. She stared at her phone on the table, wishing it would ring.

#134 – Crude Mix of Wood, Concrete, and Steel (2.21.19)

"We work our asses off all day and still have to pinch our change. Like working to be unemployed," Marcus grunted as he swung his pick into the pile of rubble; they had until the end of the week to clear the path through the most recent demolition.

"Yep, working to stay broke," Ashton agreed, swinging his pick into the crude mix of wood, concrete, and steel.

Three other men worked beside Marcus and Ashton, but they had opted against expressing their grief. Instead they muscled their way through their struggles. They may have agreed, but they couldn't bring themselves to complain.

#135 – Coal into the Master Furnace (2.22.19)

Moyan couldn't tell which discomfort affronted him more, the dehydration fever he felt from shoveling coal into the master furnace for seven hours straight or the cold that had been gradually afflicting him for the past seven weeks before that.

So he lay in the storage room between the garage and kitchen of the base.

He knew what happened to shirkers, but he would be among his fallen comrades soon enough if he didn't steal some time to rest.

He closed his eyes. Just some time to rest.

#136 – A Thousand Stars Committing Suicide (2.22.19)

Dan watched the rocket fly into the sky above the field facilitating the massive crowd; after what seemed like a blink of God, it burst into a circle of sparks that spread out like a thousand stars committing suicide.

The crowd erupted into applause, for the firework show accompanied the appearance of presidential hopeful, Maurice Blanchard.

Blanchard rode in the back of a topless Jeep, waving at his fellow citizens before hopping out of the vehicle and approaching the podium.

#137 – If the Glass Weren't There (2.23.19)

Sven relished passing the wall of windows that divided the female administrative workers from the salesmen-and-women who roved the showroom like hawks with the acumen of interested doves.

He would catch the women at their desks just across the glass, each pass eliciting a different reaction: a smile, a quick look away, as though they weren't sure how they would behave if the glass weren't there and they were faced with this pipe fitter.

Sven rounded the corner and found the office manager, who smiled with eyes like a fox.

#138 – The Last Unit (2.23.19)

"Can I help you?" she asked, her arms crossed under her chest, conveniently uplifting her breasts.

"Not particularly, I was just running out for supplies. Almost done with the upstairs unit."

"Is that the last one?"

"Yes," he answered.

"I like your accent," she noted. "Where are you from?"

"Belgium."

"Very exotic." She raised her eyebrows and smiled.

"Why don't you show me the last unit?"

He nodded and led the way.

#139 – The Itinerary of the Bill (2.23.19)

Senator Bradley regarded the latest shipment from Bellows, a diverse delivery that included stacked crates of assault rifles and ammo, pharmaceuticals, and even thirteen attack dogs, which he had overlooked in the itinerary of the bill before signing off on the order, which his staffer, Riley Burke, put together.

"Everything look good?" asked the transporter.

"Just fine," Bradley answered, stone-faced.

In these dark times, one couldn't be too sure.

#140 – In the Darkness of the Factory Basement (2.23.19)

"Do you know who my father is?" Doyle Barkley screamed in the darkness of the factory basement, his voice reverberating off the concrete floor, walls, and ceiling. "You'll never get away with this!"

Then footsteps descended the concrete stairs and a tall lean silhouette emerged from the darkness, revealing the presence of Mayor Stanford. "I know who your father is," he revealed, "and we have already gotten away with this."

Doyle regarded his godfather wide-eyed.

#141 – He Pressed on Alone (2.24.19)

Bantam entered the marble facade of the building expecting to find at least a small crowd of staffers to greet him upon arrival—which he had planned well enough in advance that the people here should have concocted some kind of welcoming ceremony.

"Hello?" His voice echoed down the deep corridor.

He decided on a direction and walked. No one occupied the lobby in the most general sense.

Disgusted, he pressed on alone.

#142 – Shock Rock Tea (2.24.19)

"We're sorry, sir—we just don't have any more Shock Rock Tea on hand," Renee said from behind the counter, forced into another uncomfortable confrontation with a customer disappointed that they had run out of the new product on the day of its release to the public.

"How the hell did you sell out? Did you undervalue your own goods? Unbelievable! Is this a communist business? Answer me, God damnit!"

"Sir—"

"Fuck this! You've lost another customer."

#143 – Privacy from the Party (2.24.19)

Greene had pulled Melinda from the party so fluidly that she didn't have a chance to ask a single question as he led her to the patio for some privacy.

Hey Nikki!

Thank you so much for checking out Bizarre Messaging, hope you enjoy ~!

Have an excellent new year,
    - JMDIII

Hey Nikki!

Thank you so much for
checking out Bizarre
Messaging, hope you enjoy
!

Have an excellent rad year)
— INUIT

She didn't know anyone at the party, but it was easy for her to mingle with new people. Greene embodied the only person she knew previously, though their relationship had trailed years ago, when she left the business and found herself a husband.

"Melinda," Greene said once they were alone. "We need you to kill your husband."

#144 – Gloomily Aside from the Gathering (2.24.19)

Jasmine sat gloomily aside from the gathering. Without Jason, she couldn't find joy anywhere, so such a congregation stood as the furthest setting for her current temperament.

She looked at her phone again, four minutes since the last time. A part of her still wanted to believe he would show or at least call. He insisted he would end the growth of his mammoth list of broken promises.

She found her friends looking at her from across the penthouse and they looked

away when they found her eyes.

#145 – The Single Most Important Space (2.25.19)

Steven gritted his teeth as he and his partner, Doug, worked their way along the long wall in the study, installing book shelving that reached from floor to ceiling.

Michelle, the designer, had insisted that the study stood as the single most important space for her client, a famous man of books.

Her insistence never ceased; she provided the third set of eyes on the scene, moving her mouth plenty while never lifting a finger to help.

"I don't know how much more of this shit I can take," Steven said to Doug when Michelle left them to take a call, to which Doug shrugged and silently pressed on.

#146 – The First Coming of True Darkness (2.25.19)

Simpson never believed a word Sonya said to him those

nights she had her way with him in her apartment, occurrences that promised paradisiacal seclusion from the busy world beyond its walls that, like everything else, made no sense to him.

They would conduct the sacrifice and bathe in its blood, freeing the first coming of true darkness unto the mortal plane, she would purr and growl.

He thought it was all part of a perversion she brought about verbally during their time alone. He was wrong.

#147 – Her Master's Chamber (2.25.19)

Ronsa slopped the rag into the soapy water bucket, wrung it out, and continued scrubbing the immaculate marble floor of her master's chamber. She attended this most sacred space at noon while he was in the capitol with the rest of the Council governing the population.

She washed with the persistence that had freed her from the city's ghetto and installed her into the capacity of the master's personal maid.

She wiped the floor, pillow under her knees.

#148 – Massive, Blocky Strides (2.25.19)

Lyon stumbled back as his opponent approached in massive, blocky strides, the cage mask obscuring his face. He moved out of the way just in time to roll away from the massive man's hands.

The spectators screamed on the other side of the octagonal barricade, chain-link fencing with three rows of barbed wire on top.

"Get back here, you little worm!"

Lyon dodged his grip again, fearing the moment his luck run out.

#149 – The Standardized Tests (2.25.19)

Mr. Klaus roamed the classroom as his students took the standardized tests. He knew who studied and who didn't, and his imaginings of each of their future prospects proved a challenge in restraining the laughter looming beneath the slack face of tight expression.

He passed Amy Crocket and her pet g-string, which she always hiked high for all to see; Bud Sandler, the jock with a brain the size of a peanut and biceps like small continents; Shay Hamaz, future bright as the sun.

#150 – Privately Transmitted Information (2.26.19)

The rioting crowds around the city reflected the public's lack of faith in the media following the recent treaty signed between their country and Russian President Atakov.

The dissemination of privately transmitted information had been criminalized a year and a half earlier, so there wasn't even material to sort through for one trying to get to the bottom of the international situation.

Police and military men were without clear instruction; disorder reigned.

#151 – "Is Everything Okay?" (2.26.19)

Thom's heart dropped when he saw the woman who opened the door. She looked just like Simona, but much, much older, looks probably surpassing her actual age.

"I uh, I can't do this," he said, running away from what he presumed to be a vision of Simona's future if he decided to pursue her.

Simona came down after he already ran down the porch. "Thom!" she called after him.

"Is everything okay?" asked Simona's mother as she entered the room, more beautiful than both her daughter and her sister.

#152 – Every Piece Has a Story (2.26.19)

"You've been looking at my necklace all night," Blondia observed once a comfortable pause arose in their conversation.

"Every piece has a story," Adin said, instinctively sipping from his glass. "Your necklace is a marvelous specimen."

A warm breeze passed over the patio. Seagulls made their presence known in the mild skies above.

"It looks like you've seen it before."

Adin reached for his gun.

"Don't. You're surrounded."

#153 – Overwhelming Constriction (2.26.19)

"Tell me more about these fears." Dr. Berkowitz wrote continuously in his notebook throughout the sessions, and added another note after he said this.

"It's more of a feeling than a vision. This overwhelming constriction, like there's a snake tightening around my throat." Juan scratched the back of his neck.

"Do you think this feeling is from within, or actually present in the world?" Berkowitz wrote on.

Juan looked up. "They're out to get me."

#154 – Set in Motion Against Him (2.26.19)

Maynard sat in his study, brow furrowed as it fully dawned on him what Vernon had set in motion against him. At first he thought it was the typical mudslinging and whispered rumors common to the halls of the Segreto Chamber. God knows, he'd slung his fair share of mud over the years, and was not prepared to be recognized as a hypocrite. But the conspiracy had coagulated within the minds of his enemies, and the only thing that shielded the full depth of their mutiny was their wall of secrecy.

#155 – The Same Vague Direction (2.27.19)

Dante walked out of the store and approached where Sante sat on the bench, facing the ocean. Dante sat beside her and fixed his attention in the same vague direction as his sister.

Without speaking, staring straight ahead, he

held out the paper bag. She looked at him and took it, then returned her gaze to the sunset.

They were alone, the sound of the surf and squawk of the gulls the only indication that the world hadn't left them behind.

"Thank you."

#156 – Eyes Scraping Like Sandpaper on Her Skin (2.27.19)

Rosa felt Jeff's eyes scraping like sandpaper on her skin each time he looked up and down at her legs. Regardless of his shameless perusals (which she had anticipated—had in fact intended, as per commands issued from the top), she had to maintain focus, find a door in his facade leading to the information they needed.

"Are you wearing a wire?" he asked in his indiscernible accent.

"Of course not. Are you?"

He smiled, satisfied with her answer.

#157 – Blast Light on His Personal Dealings (2.27.19)

Radley's bodyguards cleared the way for him as they made their way down the front stairs of the Tiogaka Building, the press pushing against him for questions and comments.

The eyes of the media people gleamed with the bloodlust of hawks, utilizing their cameras and microphones as weapons. But it was none of their business, they had no right to blast light on his personal dealings.

Radley climbed into the black SUV waiting on the street and lit his cigarette as it pulled away.

#158 – Shadow of a Contemptuous Smirk (2.27.19)

"You thought you had it all," Sienna said before lighting the long, slim cigarette inserted in the black holder. "But then I came along." She flipped her wrist to close the Zippo and dropped it into the abyss of her purse.

Benton grunted, the shadow of a contemptuous

smirk just barely losing out to the forced neutrality of his countenance. "You did come along." He spit a glob of chew. "But I ain't never thought I had it all. What is all?"

Sienna studied his eyes beneath the deep shade of his hat's brim.

#159 – Snide References in Conversation (2.28.19)

Ben gave up searching for Nona for the time being and made his way to the resort's dining area for breakfast.

He found Hill sitting at a table at a far end of the stone patio, the woman whose repulsiveness had crept into snide references in conversation with Nona the night before, causing them both to laugh before they spent hours making love.

She waved when she saw him, the extra weight on her arms flabbing in the wind.

There weren't enough people present to get away with pretending that he didn't see.

He approached, smiling cordially. "Have you seen my wife?"

"No," she said. "But why don't you join me?"

#160 – Possibility of His Culpability (2.28.19)

The men surrounding Himla with their swords unsheathed did so with great reservation, as they had previously felt nothing but respect for him.

Still, Vonta had raised grand enough charges against Himla that they could not ignore the possibility of his culpability.

Had Himla been trying to escape when they encircled him, or just milling about as per usual? It all happened so fast, not one of them knew what occurred.

#161 – Congregants of the Gathering (2.28.19)

Clario walked through the crowd feeling thoroughly dejected with the gathering— not himself. He had done his part, had spoken the truth— not *his* truth, as is so fashionable to say in modern times, but the one indisputable truth that presides over one who is honest with the tangible realities of the world.

They would all certainly turn their backs on him now.

As he would them.

#162 – The Blood Stone (3.1.19)

Araura stood at the ledge of the Hole, staring down at the Blood Stone, the crimson sphere floating within the stone cradle of the Hole, a mixture of liquid and gas swirling within its glassy membrane.

It was rumored that all the blood in the world found its way into the stone, but Araura couldn't imagine how.

She had waded through enough of it in battle to figure it mostly went to waste.

It was not her calling to deliberate.

So she pulled out her pistol and aimed.

#163 – Blinked Away the Smoke (3.1.19)

"So how did you get stuck in your current job?" O'Neil asked from behind the desk. He lit a cigarette and leaned back, causing the ancient joints of his chair to creak.

"Was my school job," McIrney answered. "Can I have one?" he requested, referring to the cigarette.

"No." O'Neil blew a stream of smoke into McIrney's face.

McIrney blinked away the smoke. He hadn't expected any kind of amenities from O'Neil's type, but he meant to find familiarity.

"Can I trust you, McIrney?"

#164 – Slammed the Door in His Face (3.1.19)

Frank opened the door when the bell rang.

"Dad!" said Junior, running inside and wrapping his arms around his father's legs, pressing the side of his face into his stomach.

"Hey, kid."

Frank mussed Junior's hair and Junior ran downstairs to play with his toys.

"You're late," Frank said to Kyle, his ex-wife's latest boyfriend, who stood on the front porch.

"Sorry, Frank—"

"Next time tell Tandy to bring Junior herself."

Frank slammed the door in Kyle's face.

#165 – Her Sleek Body (3.1.19)

Everyone gathered around Glenda when she went to the range.

As the resident ace, Glenda could cut patterns at will into her paper targets.

Not only was a she a demonic force with her arms, but her sleek body seemed a perfect human embodiment of the revolver she held so confidently in her hand.

"Damn Glenda, you sure are a heartbreaker!" Don Algene once commented when Glenda cut a heart into a human shaped target.

#166 – Silent and Unflinching (3.1.19)

The large man, silent and unflinching, led Geoff around the last corner before bringing him into the corridor of cells, Geoff yelling and crying as he put his best fight into his attempts to break free.

"Wait!" he managed, short of breath and full of fear. "I need to speak to Snooker, please!"

"Who do you think sent me to you?"

"Huh?"

The man threw Geoff to the floor and turned away. Geoff rose and found Snooker glaring at him from the shadows.

#167 – Into the Ink Jar (3.2.19)

"Come to bed," Crya urged Daniel for the seventh time in the past hour and a half.

"Soon, my dear," he said, dripping his quill into the ink jar.

"Yes, you have been saying that. Yet the night grows deep."

Daniel set his quill down and granted Crya his full attention for the first time since dinner. "Lest your selfishness abate, blood will pour through these lands like a flood."

#168 – A Ghost in a Hall of Shadows (3.2.19)

Chrystal sat at the dinner table without speaking, assuming her constant role as his trophy piece.

How the time had gone, she contemplated, a depressing consideration to sprinkle her other preoccupations, which was her wonder as to what the scores of guests at functions like these even spoke about.

She was a ghost in a hall of shadows.

Then she saw Miklos, darkness falling from his eyes from across the room.

#169 – The Shame of History (3.3.19)

Shoreside Diner had accommodated the same community for over four decades; the fluctuation in the diner's attendees owed itself mainly to deaths and births of citizens already long-planted in the town.

It was almost as though the diner and town itself were hidden from accessibility to outsiders, so scant was the appearance of an unknown face.

Same as the closed nature of the community's populous, they never forgot the shame of history.

#170 – The Ultimo Serum (3.3.19)

Henrietta struggled to keep her hand steady as she gripped the cup full of the ultimo serum. Tears streamed from her eyes as she forced herself to resist drinking from the cup, procurer of the bridge from this world, much like the

61

bridge that stood in front of her at the exit of the keep.

Marcoses should have been here by now, and she didn't want to live or die without him; did she drink the ultimo serum and cross into death, or cross the bridge into freedom?

"Henrietta!" she heard Marcoses's voice call.

#171 – Indeterminate Stretches of Time (3.3.19)

Blanche felt guilty every time she made a man cum who wasn't James, but he left her no choice when he left for indeterminate stretches of time. She commended her husband's adherence to his civic duties, but he had all but abandoned his marital obligations.

So when Larry, Kurtis, Salem, or the multitude of townsfolk came to check in on her, as they often did, she could not resist reminding someone that she was a woman, someone upon whom she could roar.

#172 – Montrose Eagles, Wyoming (3.3.19)

A gang of gunmen reportedly sacked Billy's Country Griddle of all meals cooked to completion in a feat of robbery unprecedented to the municipality of Montrose Eagles, Wyoming.

According to the footage of the three cameras covering the area the men occupied, the gang boxed meals from the kitchen as well as from the plates of dishes served to patrons in the dining area.

Before leaving, without taking a penny, one of the gunmen shot all cameras visible from where he stood at the front door.

#173 – The Southwestern Corner of Town (3.4.19)

McLaren was assigned to the southwestern corner of town for plow duty, the part of town where the streetlights shone dimmer.

He didn't have to worry about falling asleep in his constant fear that he'd get stuck in sudden gun crossfire, which was not rare in the township of Coal Valley.

Anders needs to expand his God damned staff, McLaren thought to himself, one of the only original men left.

Just then a live one went through his windshield and he had to get down—plowing would have to wait until the fight subsided.

#174 – The Criminalization of the Private Press (3.4.19)

A large man, heavy muscle on thick bone, Hendrick was not taken with the new order of things—the criminalization of the private press, and refused to oblige its strictures.

He rushed from printer to printer to make sure the antique presses wouldn't bind up as they were prone at any unexpected moment, occasionally peeking through a barn window to make sure no one was on to him.

Beside the pig trough stood the incinerator, where they burned all former editions when the readership had consumed their contents

and returned them to the printer as necessity required.

#175 – One by One Across the Valley (3.4.19)

Sheriff Bailey stood on top of Hood's Point, the highest perch overlooking Tyson's Passing, as the explosions detonated one by one across the valley.

Too stricken with disbelief to know how to act, he fell to his knees. The townspeople trusted him with their safety, and he had let them down for the last time.

All of them down there, unsuspecting victims to the scattered mushroom clouds that swallowed the municipality of his jurisdiction.

#176 – The Sweetest of Tones (3.4.19)

The lady of the house came downstairs with two glasses of iced water for the men servicing her furnace.

"Oh, much obliged, ma'am," said one, "Thank you very much," said the other.

"You boys are welcome," she said in the sweetest of tones. "We've had this thing for twenty-five years. Then one day, that was all."

The men nodded and enjoyed their refreshments.

Just then her phone rang.

"Excuse me," she answered before leaving the working men. "What the fuck is wrong with you?" she hissed into the phone as she climbed the stairs. "A simple job. I told you not to call me unless something went irreparably wrong, you twit."

#177 – Mercenaries of the Fallen World (3.4.19)

Nickenbacher sat among those gathered around the campfire, laughing as he watched three or four from among their ranks dramatizing the events comprising their raid earlier in the evening.

They may have laughed in the comfort of their campfire, but they all felt a looming dread with the prisoner they had jailed in a makeshift cell in their camp.

Their crew, mercenaries of the fallen world, were normally averse to accepting jobs involving abduction, but the client's price was right.

#178 – His Ex, Violet (3.4.19)

Butch sat at the kitchen island, one hand resting on his knee and another wrapped around the beer bottle sitting on the countertop.

He didn't know anyone there, yet had nowhere else to be that New Year's Eve, so he accepted his friend Loui's invitation to the celebration at his aunt Sabrina's house down the shore.

Dressed in a black dress shirt buttoned up to his chest, he sat trying to relax and not think about his ex, Violet.

"Why so lonesome?" Sabrina asked, drunkenly falling into him.

He caught her and said, "Who said I was lonely?

#179 – All Traces of Blood off the Floor (3.4.19)

Simon scrubbed the basement in a fury, praying that the concrete would return to its natural color once the water dried. God knows he put enough muscle into trying to get all traces of blood off the floor.

As he rounded the last stretch of his task, his phone vibrated in his pants. He took off his rubber gloves and pulled it out. His girlfriend Valerie was calling.

Simon panicked, his face, arms, and clothes being splattered with blood, but she would kill him herself if he didn't answer.

He wouldn't be doing favors for his older brother in a long time after this.

#180 – The Roar of the Arena (3.4.19)

The roar of the arena resounded into the back room, where motivational speaker Heinrich Engels prepared for his presentation. Known as a cool, collected figure to his legions of fans, he shivered with nerves before each time he went onstage.

He finally found a vein and injected what he called his "cocktail," a time-tested blend of uppers and downers, a means of temporarily cloaking the weakling he really was inside.

#181 – Crush the Intolerant (3.4.19)

"We will crush the intolerant!" Dale screamed into his megaphone, his voice cracking on "in-*tol*-er-ant".

The other protestors shouted in agreement, forming several chants at different points during the gathering.

It was a beautiful afternoon in the town center, a sunny Monday. Cars honked in their attempts to disperse the knot blocking the traffic of functional people trying to move on with their day.

"Yes, we will crush the intolerant!"

Cars honked.

65

"Hey asshole, get out of the way!" yelled one motorist through his window.

#182 – A Cleanly Life (3.4.19)

Tinsel led a cleanly life, maintaining an absolute order of all affairs. As the regional manager of four Cross State Burger locations, he had his work cut out for him, and flew mostly under the radar.

He claimed work kept him a single man, even though he summoned the best energy from all he came across.

Until the day he found detectives Joyce and Row waiting for him at one of the locations.

"Tinsel Gabbard?"

Face gone white, he nodded.

"You need to come with us."

#183 – Destroying All Tranquility in Her Path (3.5.19)

Georgina was sweet as a peach when she got what she wanted; when things didn't go her way, she could shift into a hurricane, destroying all tranquility in her path.

"Are you ready to go, darling?" she asked her husband Robin as she came down the spiral staircase into the parlor of their third home.

Robin shifted his laptop so she couldn't see the screen, which would reveal that they would be broke within days.

"Yes, sweetheart," he said, closing his computer, as she would soon do to their marriage, her third and his fifth.

#184 – The Serene Azure Waters (3.5.19)

Jacob fell to his knees in reverence before the serene azure waters of the volcano's dormant crater. Though the trees and vegetation around the lake, elevated three miles in the sky, swayed in the winds, the lake's water had remained undisturbed, as though in a state of perfect stillness for hundreds of years—at least—since the last human eyes laid eyes on its majesty.

Jacob rose to his feet, brushed the earth from his clothes, built up over the several days of his journey, and dove in, praying for salvation.

#185 – Javier Sweat Bullets (3.5.19)

Javier sweat bullets as he orchestrated the box exchange from three Chinese containers into three Mexican containers. Such a simple operation, moving the product from one nationally approved shipping unit to another, but not for a second did he forget what the consequences would be should they get caught. They depended on the isolation and thick overgrowth of the most unforgiving jungles their operation could find.

This presented the highest-risk contract they had ever taken on.

He kissed the cross hanging from his neck.

#186 – The Worst Kind of Costume (3.6.19)

Brant walked down the street as he did every day, checking the power meters of the block database of each neighborhood.

A part of him felt silly; at times his uniform felt like the worst kind of costume. He knew his duty, his colleagues and members of the communities he covered treated him with respect.

But did he respect himself? He followed his route with electronic precision, didn't even know how to round corners. Yet he didn't know what happened to the data he collected, and life became a black hole.

#187 – Representative LeBranch (3.6.19)

Representative LeBranch had an exhausting schedule—so many favors to repay, favors which landed her the seat she currently held.

She maintained a strong presence in her own district as well as her perch in D.C.

So many friends to visit, a hand to lend.

Hands to shake other hands as well as hands to pump the members of her donors.

She hoped one day to pay off her debts and begin to push the policies of her dreams.

#188 – A Blue Wall (3.6.19)

Brick tossed another handful of Brinkley Lodge chips into his mouth and scratched his nose. He had two hours to kill before the pickup. Not being very familiar with the area, he decided to go for a cruise, take in the local sites. Norman Bay was a small beach town so he took a lap down the main drag and decided to park to see the beach from his car. He found a lot and beyond the sand found a massive tidal wave approaching like a blue wall.

#189 – Deepest Chasm of the Citadel (3.7.19)

Kilroy signaled for more troops to flood from the kingdom's four gates. They needed more power to push back the united forces bent on stopping the final ritual occurring in the deepest chasm of the citadel.

Within this chamber Lau Kong, the highest-ranking Chintusa monk in the country, huddled over the scroll upon which he scrawled the new creed, an enigmatic prophecy coming to life as he wrote.

According to ancient scriptures, once the chosen monk of the final peoples drafted the last line of the future script, order would return to the land.

#190 – The Whole Charade Made Dwayne Sneer (3.7.19)

Dwayne wove through the line at the wake, comprised of relatives who despised the departed, who he despised in kind.

The whole charade made Dwayne sneer, toothpick clamped in his teeth.

He passed his stepfather's aunt, who lived down the street yet hadn't

68

spoken to her nephew in years; his stepfather's brother and next-door neighbor—who failed in pursuing a law suit against him decades ago; and his stepfather's sons and their wives, who Dwayne hadn't spoken to since the divorce, years ago.

Now, standing before the open coffin, Dwayne spat in the man's dead face.

#191 – The Orange Inferno (3.7.19)

Gran saw the fires blaze in the rearview mirror. As the orange inferno receded, the ambiguity of the future made his head spin.

He wiped the sweat from his brow, face cold to the touch.

What would he do now?

Eventually he would be foiled, but when and by whom he did not know.

He had no loved ones, and his enemies were currently being turned to ash—who would quash his personal justice?

#192 – After the Coup (3.8.19)

The men sat around the fire after the coup, friction passing through them as they experienced their success in a most unexpected light, far less exuberant and festive than they envisioned.

They were certain that their intentions were righteous—they had to be, didn't good always win in the end?

Still, the sensation remained, they all felt it, that his ghost somehow lingered among them, judging in stubborn arrogance as he always had.

#193 – Knocked the Coded Sequence (3.8.19)

Blahkman scurried down an alley in the old part of the city, the pouch Denigree entrusted him clutched tightly in his hands. He panted and wheezed as his legs stammered along. He finally reached the door of his destination and knocked the coded sequence.

The door opened a moment later, a growing crack of darkness in a world that seemed designed to blind us with its corruption.

"Did you bring it?"

"Yes," he answered, voice feeble.

#194 – Rhondai Flipped Through the Literature (3.8.19)

Rhonda flipped through the literature Danram gave him. It was all very interesting, but Rhondai was not completely sold on the group he'd heard so much about in recent months.

They had known each other since they were kids, Rhondai and Danram, but had only really gotten to know each other since they became more closely acquainted when they both started working at the local grocery store.

It started as small talk, but Danram became increasingly adamant that Rhondai join his cause.

But could he join what seemed to be a cult?

He didn't think so.

#195 – Another Administered the Tranquilizer (3.8.19)

Billyboy convulsed on the floor and Penny screamed in the terror of her confusion.

Men in sealed white suits scrambled into the room. Two held him down and another administered the tranquilizer.

They seemed to notice Penny only after Billyboy stopped moving and lost consciousness.

"What's happening?" she asked, voice saturated in fear.

"You need to come with us," said the one with the needle, his voice filtered through his face mask.

#196 – In a State of Leisure (3.9.19)

Birch made his way through the botanic swirl. From afar, one may have thought he was ambling in a state of leisure, when really he was trying to make sense of Ramsey's riddle. Birch felt dim on many matters, and this latest quandary stood as no exception. Did Ramsey come from a place of support or malevolence? Birch could make sense of none of it, and the path was only getting shorter now, looping in smaller rings. What awaited at the end of the maze?

#197 – His Lust for the Spider Queen (3.9.19)

Joomsa lay sprawled in the bed as the Spider Queen rode upon him, her wolf pack encircling them, snarling and whimpering intermittently.

He didn't know what excited him more, his fear of the wolves or his lust for the Spider Queen, the subject of countless fables.

"Think about me, only me," she said in her chorus of voices.

The wolves growled and snapped in their ring around them, moving closer.

"Me, not them."

#198 – The Deterioration Process (3.10.19)

The deterioration process began with his mind, so

following the initial shock there was no surprise when he lost control of his limbs and eventually saw them blow away with the digital winds of the future as particles of sacrificial dust.

Eventually his eyes were buried beneath the debris of a revolution that left the world in a worse place than before all the wars began.

He had enough sense left to ask one final question: did he even want the veil of earth removed from his eyes?

#199 – The Wintry Woods (3.10.19)

Lance and Lou allowed a rare note of seriousness to ring through their conversation on their walk home from the bus stop. They had grown up next-door neighbors, honorary brothers. Nothing had occurred in either of the twelve-year-olds' lives without the other knowing.

"My brother says politics are fake, we're slaves no matter what," Lou said.

"My dad feels that way," Lance said, kicking a small stick down the street.

71

"It's not worth divorcing over."

"I know," Lance agreed, picking up the stick and throwing it into the wintry woods.

#200 – As the Future Spoke (3.11.19)

Gowdy crept through the cave, guided by the lick of sunlight dancing on the shallow waters of the underground creek.

Gowdy put in his share with the others regarding settlement duties, but he wasn't prone to wasting his earnings on gambling and the traveling brothel—he intended to expand and took liberty to keep his private investigations to himself.

He walked down the cave until sunlight was no more and lit his lantern, setting the walls ablaze with gold and flame as the future spoke.

#201 – Some Ghosts Remain under Lease to Their Earthly Treasures (3.11.19)

Within the forgotten crypt the battle sword stood vertically in the center of the chamber—the first thing Gowdy saw as the torch brought the darkness to life.

He approached with caution, knowing not to dismiss the possibility that some ghosts remain under lease to their earthly treasures.

No spirits avenged him, however, and he pulled the battle sword from its sheathing mound of gold.

He turned the sword to and fro, the fire's reflection speaking of true inferno on its blade.

#202 – Another Grunt Job without a Tip (3.11.19)

Gabton climbed into his van, threw the paperwork onto the dashboard, and started the engine. He cursed the customer; another grunt job without a tip. He backed the van out of the driveway and pulled over a few houses down the street.

He filled the cannabis chamber with a handful of weed and engaged the vehicle's internal vaporizer. He pulled the hose from its holder and took a massive rip of the vapor.

Before exhaling, he shifted the van into gear and followed his GPS toward the next job, puffing all the way.

#203 – All the Monotony and Hourless Days (3.11.19)

Tinson ripped his blade down the center of a large sheet of cardboard. He then folded each half and stuffed it in the cardboard compactor. This was his life, the monotonous duty they assigned him. All day he had to fill the compactor, bail it when it was filled, and continue the process until his warden labor manager told him it was mealtime or when his shift was over (timekeeping during work hours was illegal in his sector).

Tinson knew no better, had never seen better, never imagined that anything could

be better; it was all monotony and hourless days.

#204 – Pressed to the Wall (3.12.19)

Sheila Owens made her way down the corridor with her back pressed to the wall, both hands clasped over her pistol.

The fluorescent lights went in and out, more out than in, and she could feel her heart thumping in her ears.

Sweat poured from her face, slicked her arms and shoulders, but the mild discomfort of the itch paled to her fear of the roaming things.

A figure rounded the corner and she fired the gun.

She screamed when she realized she'd shot a mortal.

#205 – Into the Herd (3.11.19)

Meltem accompanied Boyle for a stroll through the herd system. They walked on elevated networks of walkways as the bison roamed the maze of the facility. Communications

73

between their respective factions had soured in recent months, and Meltem feared that their meat deal was under threat.

They had both been involved in clan politics for a long time, and Meltem expected an exchange of pleasantness.

Instead, without warning, Boyle pushed him over the railing into the herd.

#206 – Faded and Cracked Like His Own (3.13.19)

Morton Shields knotted his tie in front of the same mirror that stood in his bedroom for the past six decades, its finish faded and cracked like his own.

If Miranda were still alive he would find her in the kitchen at this point of the morning, standing at the counter as she made his breakfast.

But she wasn't, and he constantly needed to find new things to look forward to.

He'd paid his dues in work.

He'd had his share of women.

Maybe he needed to die to feel comfortably alone.

#207 – He Had No Good Reason (3.13.19)

Kirk prayed to find Morticia outside every time he had to mow the lawn. His parents didn't ask much of him, and he had no good reason to deny them this single chore.

Seeing his next-door neighbor only served to incentivize the task.

On the day in question fate served him well and he found her sitting at her patio table, facing the lawn Kirk mowed.

Kirk wore sunglasses, and could not tear his eyes off Morticia with each lap.

On the next lap he saw her smiling at him, dressed in her characteristic black dress and sheer veil.

#208 – The Late Afternoon Heat (3.14.19)

Carrie stood on the roof of the Millstone Cinema, looking down at the constant flow of traffic passing through the center of town. The late afternoon heat enveloped her and she felt like she was melting.

Tears welled in her eyes, and she stepped onto the ledge, the same ledge she and Andrew sat on so many times.

Then she heard shouting below.

"I told you to watch your—"

The words were cut off by the sound of a gunshot.

#209 – Feeling Like Iron Weights (3.14.19)

Jeremy could focus on nothing other than the lines on the road and the act of keeping his eyes open, the lids feeling like iron weights. He didn't know how many more jobs he could take; life had become a repetitive routine of stops leading to nowhere but the next depot.

He drank a swig of the crank, an illegal sleep suppressant, and gripped the wheel with both hands, trying to steady his focus.

Another thirty-six-hour drive to add to his directionless path.

#210 – Uninvited Guests Expected to Enter without Knocking (3.15.19)

Jamal sat on one of the couches in the large area of the house designated as the living room. The couch was positioned before the large flat screen TV the Bensons used, but he was more interested in the snow falling outside. He had never seen snow before, and figured this was just as good an opportunity to experience the broader seasons beyond the Caribbean island dots that raised him.

But he wasn't here to vacation like the Bensons, who vacationed in the Caribbean.

Instead, gun resting in his lap, he was assigned to wait for uninvited guests expected to enter without knocking first.

#211 – The Subbasement of the Lab (3.15.19)

Jordan converted the panic he felt when he discovered what Kobach was doing in the subbasement of the lab into stone cold resolve to free the subjects of an experiment spanning several decades. Techs and directors were prone to scurrying through the facility, so his haste turned no heads.

He managed to hail an elevator and dropped to the building's lowest level.

He reached the containment chamber detailed in the report he found accidentally on Kobach's desk and gasped at the sight of the dozens of deformed and malnourished individuals who awaited him.

#212 – From the Opening in the Bedroom (3.16.19)

"Just tell me who the hell he is," Carlos demanded from the opening in the bedroom.

"Carlos, you need to drop this now," Rosha said in a tight voice, breaking the silence she upheld since he confronted her in their chamber.

"Please," he pleaded, dropping to his knees at her feet and taking her hands in his own. "Don't let us fall apart."

Rosha pulled her hands free and continued packing her chest.

"You've had your chances." Rosha closed the chest. "And have only lifted a finger when it was already too late."

#213 – The Serpent Throne (3.16.19)

Silvo sat beside the Snake Queen, who occupied the Serpent Throne, clad scantily in her snakeskin wear.

She turned to him and smiled, then returned her gaze to the feeding taking place in the center of the throne room, where Silvo's uncle screamed as the beasts tore him to shreds.

Silvo squirmed.

An invitation from the Snake Queen stood as an order—all knew this, and she had invited him to witness a capital feasting.

"Now you know what shall happen to you if you betray me, as your uncle has before you."

Soon the beasts had devoured his uncle's face to

expose the yellow bone beneath.

#214 – An Anachronism (3.16.19)

Jerry Ashton sat defeated in the chair across the desk from his literary agent, Sheila Morgan. Dressed in his faded tweed suit, Jerry couldn't have felt more like an anachronism.

"I'm sorry, Jerry." Sheila dropped Ashton's manuscript on the desk before him. "I can't do anything with this."

This stood as the third manuscript he'd admitted in the past two years. Since replacing his deceased agent, Albert Carny, Sheila had not accepted a single submission.

"The world seems to have moved on," she told him. "I'm sorry, Jerry."

#215 – The Youth Compound (3.16.19)

Kyla held out the chalice of the youth compound. "Drink, now."

Daniel shriveled deeper into the overstuffed armchair

they transported from venue to venue for him on tour. "I can't anymore," he said, more weaselly than anticipated.

"You must. You made a deal."

"But they trust me," he said, biting his fingernails. "I can't betray them anymore— they need me!"

"No one trusts you," Kyla corrected. "They pay you mind because you drink their blood. Drink, now."

Feebly, he accepted the chalice and drank.

#216 – The Swamp People (3.16.19)

Richard had been dressed in the style of the swamp people since the day they captured him, but for the life of him he could find no path toward assimilation.

It took him days until he could bring himself to trust their food.

Now, three months later, dressed in a grungy loin cloth, he watched as his captors performed their nightly spirit dance around the fire.

Surprising himself most of all, he entered the ring of dancers and broke into the steps he'd absorbed through watching.

Shedding their own surprise, the natives laughed and danced alongside him.

#217 – Stared at the Wayward Student in Disbelief (3.16.19)

Jameson stared at Principal Sanders from across the desk in the latter's office.

"What do you have to say for yourself?" Sanders asked him when he finished recounting the allegations against Jameson, an unmistakable threat in his delivery.

"I don't know," Jameson said in his lighthearted fashion. "I should ask you the same."

"About what?"

"Don't be stupid, Sanders. I hacked your computer, copied the entire hard drive. I'd say you have more to worry about than I do."

Sanders dropped his pen and stared at the wayward student in disbelief.

#218 – In the Clearing Where They Set Up Camp (3.16.19)

Strosse strode through the sewer hunched over and defeated after finding his entire regiment slaughtered in the clearing where they set up camp.

Perhaps what assailed him could be considered misery, a sensation he'd never experienced before.

He had brute strength but no great memory, could scarcely remember events that occurred mere hours earlier. Yet as far as his memory could see, his brothers occupied his mind's eye.

He feared he would never find their killers, which drove the wedge deeper into his heart.

#219 – A Schooled Lady of High Society (3.16.19)

Madame Ringer lived as Mortis Englin's loyal wife for a decade and a half, had arrived on his doorstep as a country bumpkin, and wound up a schooled lady of high society.

That was his perception, anyway. He would never suspect that she was a mole installed by a rivaling clan, that her ordained purpose in life was to ensure his fall.

The night she poisoned him she cleaned their house out of habit and to keep herself busy until she was to be retrieved.

#220 – Myriads of Clientele (3.17.19)

Lordes Clay saw her boss, Herald Trevale, as the end all be all of the professional world that inhabited their sort, a mogul where any legal, media, and political needs converged for an all-purpose service for their myriads of clientele.

She stood by his side even through all the scandal and controversy that orbited around him like planets around stars. She knew he appreciated her in his own way, but theirs was a relationship of efficiency and a shared thirst for power.

Her only exclusion presented itself in her lack of invitation to the gentlemen retreat to his Caribbean island.

#221 – The School Her Group Occupied (3.17.19)

Tasha paced in the gymnasium of the school her group occupied.

Joshua entered and watched her from the doorway.

"What do you want?" she asked when she saw him.

"Listen, Tasha—"

"Stop," she said, flinching when she heard the pleading tone in his voice.

"How was I supposed to tell you?" he asked, replacing the pleading with authority.

"Leave me alone," she said, her back to him, her life turned upside down in a moment's revelation while Daniel and a handful of others were on the road.

#222 – A Broad Smile (3.17.19)

Marcia wore a broad smile on her face as she carried the tray, her arm bent at a perfect angle. She delivered the drinks to the VIP rooms that still had the green lights shining above their doors.

Like most employees of the establishment, The Gray Mark, desperation delivered her to its door, a promise of hellfire cloaked in gold.

She knew what occurred behind closed doors in the VIP rooms once the lights above the doors shone red, a truth which could be ignored only with a smile.

#223 – A Perfectly Arranged Pattern (3.17.19)

Panchent stood on top of the tallest hill on his property as the men below dug holes in a perfectly arranged pattern across the field.

His sister, Ariella, ran up from behind, sobbing. "How could you do it?" She punched his chest with the bottoms of her fists.

He pulled her into his arms and ran his hand through her hair. "I didn't do it," he said. "I found a better way."

She pulled her head away. "How?"

Just then, lines of men appeared up a smaller hill in the distance carrying tiny trees of life.

#224 – Hiding in the Open (3.18.19)

Tonka stood outside the bunker. He could hear several stoneworkers chiseling their slabs on the other side of the building, but he was alone, hiding in the open.

He cleared his throat and spit on the dry red sand. He had lived among Gregor for two years now with no inkling of the man's crimes, crimes directly impacting his own life—hiding in the open, as he now did himself.

The only thing Tonka didn't know was whether Gregor knew that Tonka was part of the kin Gregor brutalized.

Either way, he would serve his enemy the

vengeance burning in his heart.

#225 – Slipped into the Skill Like a Glove (3.18.19)

Julie smiled with youthful openness as she held onto the rope that towed her in the wake of Gerard's ski boat. Today began her love for water skiing, but within a half dozen attempts she slipped into the skill like a glove.

Gerald smiled his movie star smile, minding the water ahead as well as Julie's progress on the rope.

Trent, Julie's boyfriend, eyed Gerald suspiciously. He took a quick swig of beer and wiped his mouth.

"Quite a girl you've got," Gerald commented. "Do you want to try?"

"I'll pass," Trent said curtly, taking another swig.

#226 – Thoughts of His Next Task (3.19.19)

Chad left the warehouse distracted with thoughts of his next task when Ra jumped him from behind.

"You ain't a fuckin' man, you snitch!" he screamed.

An inexperienced fighter, Chad swung blindly up at Ra and managed to make a firm connection with his jaw. Ra stepped back, apparently not expecting a reaction to the sneak attack.

"Be a man and do your God damned job," Chad said, spitting before making his way toward the shop.

#227 – Eating Somewhat Arrogantly (3.19.19)

Monda sat straight on her chair at the dining table. Brahn sat across from her, in her opinion eating somewhat arrogantly, an external expression of his sense of total ownership.

"How is your father?" he asked. He dabbed his mouth and took a sip of red wine.

Brahn and Monda's father had been friends for years; now he basked in her maturity as they dined in private.

In her glimmering dress, she said, "Let's not talk about my father."

#228 – Sea of Leather and Blood (3.19.19)

From a sea of leather and blood, a hand broke free to grasp the air in the world above the bodies.

Sophie crawled out of the pile gasping, spitting death from her mouth.

She knew everyone in her regiment by name, but now their souls had been stripped from their bodies, reduced to clothed flesh.

Her memory told her what happened; her mind refused to accept it. Whatever it was, she prayed it was far from here by now.

She chose a direction and walked.

#229 – The Foot of His Masters' Bed (3.19.19)

Binbin slept at the foot of his masters' bed at night, and around the house while they were at work to afford the roof that protected them from the sky at night. He couldn't speak to them, couldn't make demands. All he could do was purr and nudge, snuggle close to express his affection. The man woke first, and the black cat followed him around like a puppy until he walked out the door to start his day. Then he jumped into the bed and curled up close to the woman until it was time for her to leave him, too.

#230 – In the Aftermath (3.20.19)

Cranston sat on his stool at the bar feeling that he was the only person in the establishment, though he was surrounded by his team and so-called friends, who basked more in his victory than he did himself.

What sense of victory could he really feel? The gig was rigged, the first time he partook in such an operation.

In the aftermath of everything, he suspected this was not the end of it; he imagined Evergreen to be sitting around moping and expecting full vengeance.

#231 – Freeing Flowing Brunette Locks (3.21.19)

Cherie Kerwin, the social farce, pulled off her headset as she walked backstage. Her gleaming smile, the prize of the populous, dropped from her face like a lead weight once the audience was behind her. She pulled her hair tie from her bun, freeing flowing brunette locks.

"Darison, where is my fucking coffee?" she called above the bustle of the crew, who were desensitized to the underlying boorishness of one of the age's most moral minds.

Darison appeared like a skittish dog. "Here's your coffee, Cherie."

#232 – In His Penthouse Apartment (3.22.19)

Morrison Sinclair sat wrapped in a plush white robe on the living room couch in his penthouse apartment, a glass of expensive scotch in his hand.

It was his job to act like the interests of those who filled his coffers were on the constant rise, yet off-set the magnates bore into him with blame for the network's failing ratings.

Still firing on full cylinders from the previous night's show, he had since been laid off, with no public statement to be made or comment offered by the network's other anchors.

#233 – This Season of Eternal Darkness (3.24.19)

Magisko sprung to consciousness with a start. Panting, he rose to his feet and ran to the window of his chamber to look out into the night sky. Based on the sky's cloud density and depth of blackness, he ascertained that he must have been asleep for several days.

In this season of eternal darkness, one could be forgiven for losing track of the hours when the same pitch could represent any given day or night if one didn't track the clouds.

No one had summoned him in these days of slumber, so peace held the keep.

#234 – To Paint Even an Outline (3.24.19)

Trains had been made forbidden in the district in which Romb lived since before he was born, and he hadn't heard enough about them from those who lived before the ban to paint even an outline of what he should come to expect in the event that he see one, let alone ride in one of its cars as he did now.

Despite the wonder that encapsulated him, he regarded the train's other passengers with suspicion.

There was no telling who among him could be after the information contained in the satchel held close to his chest.

#235 – All the Operations that Occurred in the Facility (3.24.19)

Dr. Montrose used his nurse, Miss Darling, who was actually in charge of all the operations that occurred in the facility, as a proxy-facilitator of comfort in the moments leading to whatever procedure Dr. Montrose was to undertake.

"It will all be over soon," Miss Darling would say in her most soothing tones as the doctor prepared the syringe.

She always managed to garner the trust of the subject, even if she alone stood on the summit of hierarchy.

#236 – The Concrete Labyrinth (3.24.19)

There were three quicksand vats in the massive furnace room, a silently deafening hum pervading the concrete labyrinth that encapsulated them.

The Longley Company disposed of "dispensable elements" by means of throwing them into these quicksand vats, at the bottom passing through a grinding system that reduced them to pulp to be extracted later to fuel the machines.

And the machines were always hungry.

#237 – Its Black Snake Tongue (3.24.19)

Skillman stood with a handful of lab techs as they stared at their find, an unknown variety of mammal discovered on the ice cap the base had built upon. Standing on two hind legs and carrying other vague humanoid features, the specimen also carried characteristics of canine, feline, reptile, and bird varieties.

"What the hell is it?" Skillman said, not asking anyone present in particular.

Then it blinked and stuck out its black snake tongue.

#238 – The Dark Corridor of Contemptuous Cunning (3.25.19)

Dwayne Passage stood as a rugged, handsome picture of masculine durability from yesteryear. In the current year, Dwayne presented a social pariah. Where his smile would have once conjured trust and amiability in another time, a tour into the fine arts of charisma, it now provoked the deepest suspicions from those among him, a slow cruise down the dark corridor of contemptuous cunning.

"Hello, Dorothy," he greeted his secretary, wearing his brightest smile.

"Your 9AM is waiting in your office," she said with a face twisted in disdain.

#239 – The Darkh Agency (3.25.19)

Renauld thought the Darkh Agency was a gift from heaven when they first courted him, when they filled him with promises of posterity and influence, convinced him that his judgment would satiate the needs of all who lived in the district, down to the hardest calls that would lead to justified execution.

A little over a year into his new position and his full-fledged faith in the organization, and his role in particular, had dwindled like withering roses under desert sunlight.

How many lives had he destroyed, and for what? And

he had only met his quote once, after his first month.

#240 – The Clearview Mill (3.25.19)

They gave Clifford one job: to watch the entrance of the Clearview Mill, the main source of lumber for four counties. He was not to allow anyone entry—first by means of persuasion, then by physical means, if necessary.

Clifford was not a bright young man, but his task was clear as day in his mind. His keepers, old man Montgomery Gaston and his three sons, slightly more developed man-children than Clifford himself, considered the simpleton a virtuoso of his task, as no one ever discovered what happened after hours at the mill.

#241 – Somewhat Electrifying the Room (3.26.19)

Draskyll leaned back against the opening. Dora Moreira, wife of sugar cane magnate, Javier Moreira, sat in a chair beside the window looking out at the bay. Wind rustled through the open window, somewhat electrifying the room.

"Why are you here?" Dora asked Draskyll without turning his way, finding more interest in the moonlight dancing on the water.

"It's been three days," Draskyll said, voice hesitant.

"I don't care." Dora refused to turn toward him. "Do your job and don't come back here.

#242 – Soaked in Sweat (2.27.19)

"Would you like a glass of water?" asked agent Mandy McGreeny.

Soaked in sweat after hours of questioning, Troy Avelson nodded vigorously.

"I'm sure you do." Mandy nodded. "But we need you to start cooperating. We haven't been making any progress."

"I'm trying," Troy pleaded. "But I really don't know what happened that night."

"That's a shame," Mandy said. "All that water going to waste."

#243 – Beyond the Reach of the Streetlight (3.27.19)

Damien stood across the street from the local government building, obscured by the shadows just beyond the reach of the streetlight standing between him and the highly anticipated meeting transpiring within.

He still hadn't decided whether to go through with his plan, but at least he had physically placed himself in position to make such a decision.

Then he heard the muffled pop of gunshots inside the building and a herd of screaming people spilled from the building.

#244 – Those of Nondisclosure Among Them (3.28.19)

Teagan left the meeting in tears. Now she understood why they waited until after she signed the long stack of contracts, those of nondisclosure among them, to relay the most unpalatable details of her new position.

The office workers beyond Black's office door shed not a second glance at her in her crumpled state; surely they had grown accustomed to such displays.

She retreated into a stairwell and sat on the top step, holding her hand over her mouth to muffle her sobs.

#245 – A Knife Cutting Through Butter (3.28.19)

Harvey watched the girl run across the five-lane highway like a knife cutting through butter, as though it was the most natural thing in the world, her thousandth time.

He turned to his daughter in the passenger seat, distracted by whatever flowed from her ear pods, and considered how she could never traverse the world in the way of the street girl, who was dressed almost tactically in her cargo pants and tightly fitted green denim jacket.

He wondered if she felt the risk with the things she did without a second thought.

#246 – When the Capitalists Overreached (3.30.19)

Ringus Olfain represented a pinnacle of morality to his half of society. He always knew just what to say when the capitalists overextended their reach, when the conservatives presented any degree of reaction to their progressive idealism.

That had been the past thirty years.

No more.

Even the tentacles of his representatives in the press could not or were not willing to coverup for him any longer.

He now sat in a prison of his own hypocrisy.

#247 – A Cacophony of Horns and Screeching Tires (4.1.19)

Klenchaw threw the car into a lower gear and roared around the corner, prompting a cacophony of horns and screeching tires through the humid city night.

Dagney sat tensely in the passenger seat, her eyes shooting nervously across the car, though she knew better than to speak.

How differently things had become in the past several months that they had gotten close.

How deep into madness the gentleman had descended.

#248 – A Proper Cigar (4.1.19)

Grumple exhaled a massive plume and ashed his blunt, so thick and well rolled that it could easily have been mistaken for a proper cigar.

"Will you help me?" Shana asked, glaring at him impatiently through the smoked-out den.

Grumple studied her, playing with his beard as he contemplated her dilemmas. "I don't think you need my help."

"I do."

"You can't afford it."

"I can."

#249 – A Mutual Acquaintance (4.1.19)

"Mr. Marcels is one of our best clients," Sidney Oshkosh said glowingly in her sweet Southern drawl as the prospective client who sat across the table mentioned those who may present a mutual acquaintance.

"Very interesting," said McDermitt, the man currently shopping her services. He sipped from his black coffee, eyeing her suspiciously. "Mr. Marcels and Mr. Vega have gone missing recently."

Fear seemed to bolt through Sidney, and she pursed her lips. "Are you a police officer?"

McDermitt pulled out his badge and placed it on the table.

#250 – The Bridge of Blades (4.1.19)

Treinus walked the bridge of blades, thousands of knives interlocked in an arch over the water realm, the fathomless pool of black liquid.

The knives levitated on the grounds of mutual trust, their shared motivations transcending all preconceived notions of physics.

He reached the halfway point and found Inseis waiting as planned.

"Have you fulfilled your end of our deal?"

Treinus held out the sack by its drawstring, reluctantly releasing it as Inseis pulled it from his hands.

#251 – The Green World (4.1.19)

Gray slipped deeper into the green world as his friends scurried to find a key to get him out.

His face paled in his helplessness, though it could not be said that he experienced any degree of fear. In his acceptance of his hopeless condition, he waited to see which road fate would follow once it pushed beyond the fork where he stood.

Feelings faded from his fingers as the backdrop of this

dimension seeped over the canvas of the forefront.

#252 – Cathedral of Empty Darkness (4.2.19)

Tommy walked over the checkered tiles in a chosen direction, which didn't matter because the room was so deep one could not see a wall any which way.

Looking down, he felt that he was walking on water, his boots sending ripples with each step.

"Hello?" he called, his voice echoing in the cathedral of empty darkness.

He knew an answer would never come, but he stepped on, continued to pine for a divine sign.

#253 – Thick Horns Protruding from Their Helmets (4.3.19)

Kieran sat across the round table from the council leader, Byson, flanked by his top advisors, all of them masked in the traditional wear, thick horns protruding from their helmets.

Kieran still didn't know why he was here. He had just come with the woman when she asked him to. A checkpoint in the past, the origin of this new future, which began as a day off and a morning spent at a local coffee shop that veered into the unknown in a limo that delivered him to where he was now.

Now the woman was a distant memory.

#254 – A Calling into a Broader Narrative (4.3.19)

"Is anyone sitting here?"

Kieran looked up, hypnotized from the moment he looked into her eyes; a hypnosis of ambiguous origin, as he felt nothing personal floating between them, more of a calling into a broader narrative.

"No," he said, gesturing to the empty seat across the table.

She sat.

He didn't know how, but an engrossing conversation arose between them. She laid out a cryptic cause that he found himself subscribing to.

Eventually she led him to the limo and the rest was history.

#255 – Candidate Murdock Wilson (4.3.19)

Mobay sat in silence as the inmates around him cheered with each talking point presidential candidate Murdock Wilson delivered to the cameras. The man, a serving senator, spoke of lifting many crimes from the jurisdiction of incarceration, platitudes casting waves of relief through the millions behind bars who had been put away for the listed crimes.

Mobay knew his depth of crime could not be reconciled in the face of Wilson's wildest proposals, and regarded those among him who cheered with contempt.

#256 – This Population of Lawless Miscreants (4.3.19)

Maranda lay in her cell's small cot too afraid to sleep every night. She couldn't decide who posed a bigger threat, the other women in the facility or the guards charged with maintaining the rule of law among this population of lawless miscreants.

Everyone said they were innocent, sometimes with an ironic laugh reminiscent of an eye roll.

But Maranda really was innocent, and wanted to remain so, despite those who surrounded her with their evil.

#257 – Through the Wooden Slats (4.3.19)

Kenny Apricott stood with his body pressed against the fence as he peered through the wooden slats separating his family's lawn from the Conway's.

Mrs. Conway spent at least twenty minutes a day in her backyard jacuzzi, fully nude. He would watch her every day if he could, but he had impediments such as baseball practice and karate.

As he stared through the fence, he imagined Mrs. Conway leaving her husband

and children and taking him away, far from his parents.

#258 – The Iron Will of Its Pilot (4.4.19)

The borg suit, standing fifteen feet tall, would remain motionless if not for the iron will of its pilot, the handicapped Lewis Furroughs, whose consciousness had been bypassed from its broken shell of flesh and blood into the exoskeleton of thick steel that crossed the wasteland of infrastructure and machinery that floored the earth of the present day, a mausoleum of progress, a cemetery of civilization.

#259 – A Map of Worms (4.4.19)

Wendy couldn't stop staring at the veins in the man's face, like a map of worms slithering across his forehead and down his cheeks, a nest of activity beneath his skin.

His attention seemed set on a distant realm of thought, so she didn't bother hiding her awe of his physiology.

He had come upon their alley like a prophet, delivering a sermon of blood, fire, and brimstone in his mellow voice, a conscious beyond.

As his congregation grew, so did the vein-work of his face.

#260 – An Operating Room Hospital Bed (4.4.19)

He stared at the city's glow through the curtains of the massive rosette window in the attic, the streetlights outside bleeding through the stained glass like blood on an operating room hospital bed.

His assistants cut the mold from the bread as he waited for some kind of sign, anything he could bring to his disciples.

Sometimes he perceived something, other times he didn't; ultimately though, he never promised frequency or accuracy.

#261 – He Did the Lord's Work (4.4.19)

They gathered around the front door like children awaiting their father to return from work. He was out in the world, which meant inside the brick building they called the Shrine. This reversal of concept flourished because all other than the prophet and his assistants were confined to the outdoors, rain or shine, snow or hurricane. For he did the Lord's work, the unnamed one, and they did not dare question his agency. So they waited for him to appear with a message, the sight of his veined face the only thing that could placate their need for divinity.

#262 – A Unification of Marginalization (4.6.19)

Alva hated her parents for bringing her to this new country. The sidelong looks, the sensation of being seen as an outsider. There were many like her among their district, and at first she felt a camaraderie between them, a unification of marginalization.

She still hated her parents, but her view of the situation had evolved. Constant brutality within her native country pervaded news-boxes across the globe, yet she'd never experienced violence here.

Violence around the world had escalated as of late, and she wondered if she shot sidelong glances of her own.

#263 – A Guard Brought Her to the Meeting Area (4.6.19)

Amy hated the entire staff at the Einstone Institute for reasons unique unto each employee she met. If not for her brother, Jarrett, she would never have needed to acquaint herself with such a place.

After filtering through the security checks, a guard brought her to the meeting area.

Jarrett joined her a few moments later. Dressed in his white jumpsuit, face growing out of his neck, he sat across the table from her. "You came," he said, voice low and watery.

"I did," she said, looking down at her hands.

#264 – Dressed More Appropriately for a Funeral (4.7.19)

Aubrey stood alone at a far corner of the lawn, aloof to the family reunion that had entered full swing not too long ago.

Dressed more appropriately for a funeral, despite the generous glimpses of skin at her thighs.

"I hate them, too," said a pale young boy around the age of six.

Aubrey couldn't contain the small smirk the boy summoned to her lips. She kneeled down to speak to him eye to eye. "And what might your name be?"

"Embryo."

#265 – Like a Pinball from Man to Man (4.8.19)

Charlie enjoyed building sand castles.

That was about the only thing he liked about the desert, where his mother bounced from man to man in her quest for security in this post-civilized world.

Charlie would build castle after short-lived castle.

All the men treated him well, never like he was their own son.

He eventually came to see her as the crazy one among the chaos that surrounded him.

#266 – Intravenous Adrenaline Supplements (4.8.19)

When his aids finished injecting him with his intravenous adrenaline supplements, he drank the steadying compound. The makeup artists wiped the sweat from his face, sprayed a mist of antiperspirants, and set to work on prepping him for the event.

He refused to speak before hitting the stage, and was known to fire people on the spot if they broke his concentration while he prepared for a performance.

When given the silent gesture from his manager, he

stood, buttoned the top button of his jacket, and entered to rabid applause.

#267 – A Washing Machine/Dryer (4.8.19)

Lloyd was prepared to buy his wife, Mika, a washing machine/dryer set, but she considered conducting such activities at home as antisocial. Instead, she opted to do the laundry at the same laundromat she had used for the past seven years, Perry's Laundry. Lloyd shook his head; she could do whatever she pleased. So while she went out to wash their clothes, he sat on his recliner in tighty whities, a bottle of beer held loyally in his hand as he watched the game on the living room TV.

#268 – Being Flat Broke (4.8.19)

Gregor left the interview, his third so far that week (a hot Tuesday at the beginning of April) with his head slumped in defeat.

Each potential employer provided words of encouragement, but he knew that it would all end the same.

Being flat broke, he went straight home, even though his stomach grumbled in heavy hunger.

Katya noticed the failure on his face the moment he walked in the door and proceeded to upend the kitchen, as she was prone.

#269 – The Masters of the Battlefield (4.8.19)

The masters of the battlefield had lost their burden of guilt many wars ago as they moved the pieces, small figurines cut from wood, across the board.

They all knew what the slightest move one of the pieces represented.

One piece represented hundreds of thousands of lives.

Should the wrong move be made, any number of souls from those totals could perish in bloodshed.

The next master in the circle pushed his figure into a mountain range on the board, unsure how his decision would specifically affect his masses.

#270 – A Balcony Built into the Pyramid's Side (4.8.19)

Riley eventually came to feel at home in the pyramid where Hussein brought him. They would spend the sunset moments on a balcony built into the pyramid's side. From their vantage point it looked like the desert sands were ablaze beneath the sun's authority.

"They will rewrite history as they wish," Hussein told Riley, neither of them looking away from the burning earth. "All we can do is hold on to what we know, not succumb to their will."

Riley nodded, trying somehow to see through the flames.

#271 – The Grand Tome of Terror (4.8.19)

Gerard and Sally would choose one story a night from the anthology, the grand tome of terror they regarded as a bible to provide meaning to the husks of their lives.

Though they had each read the book through several times, they would choose a selection and regard it as new.

They eventually came to memorize the words on the pages, internalize them, and enact them in the world at large, no matter the casualties, and always get away with it.

#272 – Anchors of the Late-Night News (4.8.19)

"These fucking idiots," Frank said in his booming tone as the anchors of the late-night news struggled to cope with the embarrassing revelation of the latest hoax that rocked the nation.

"Psh, don't get me started," scoffed Frank's brother, Vinnie.

Junior, who sat in the corner playing with his wooden blocks, had never known political conversation to pervade family interaction, but within the past two years, contention of opinion had destroyed the marriages of both Frank and Vinnie, who had joined forces to purchase the condo.

#273 – An Uncountable Sum of Squatters (4.9.19)

"Wake me when it's over."

Before he could object, Shayanna fell into Morton's lap, submitting to sleep as soon as she closed her eyes.

Bombs exploding outside the officially vacated tenement building, which housed an uncountable sum of squatters, shook the earth.

They had travelled across most of the country, which had been fire bombed into oblivion with nary a structure left standing. Finally they had found this paradise of dilapidated cityscape, and now it was being revoked like the rest.

#274 – An Irredeemable Sinner (4.9.19)

On the streets, the collective voice of society decried the killer as an irredeemable sinner, a great disrupter of civic order.

The city had never seen such violence as it had that summer, when a thirst for violence seemed to rise from the depths of hell itself, and the population began to protest daily, although there were no suspects to deliver to the gallows.

Beyond the eyes of the prying world, however, the killer spent his days screaming, crying, and vomiting, dwelling in a suffering that none among the living could understand.

#275 – The Grounds of Her Family's Estate (4.9.19)

Sauré loved to roam the grounds of her family's estate. She knew all the workers by name, a quality they all greatly admired and appreciated.

With the string of murders rolling out across the city beyond the fortification that insulated the family mansion, she recognized the security that her class alone enjoyed.

She thought she saw a shooting star in the sky, standing on a balcony looking over the city on the night in question, but realized it was a flair thrown by a protestor.

#276 – The Package's Final Destination (4.9.19)

She retrieved the package from the homeless man, or so she still assumed him to be, and then proceeded with her route on foot, chilly rain splashing over her feet as she clicked down the pavement, now passing beneath a footbridge that circled over the path she walked through the park.

Soon she entered the quiet neighborhood where the package's final destination stood in a row of old townhouses.

She knocked on her handler's door. It creaked open, the darkness of the house's interior obscuring the face of the man who greeted her.

"Thank you," he said in his Eastern European accent, accepting the package before closing the door.

#277 – The Filthy Package Glowing with Grime in His Hands (4.9.19)

Boris closed the door behind him and made his way upstairs, the filthy package glowing with grime in his hands.

When he entered the bedroom, he looked up and found Vishna standing before him with a revolver gripped tightly in her hands.

"Vishna," he said, as a question and possibly a measure to reassure himself of his own presence. "What are you doing?"

"Toss it to me," she whispered, face red, gun shaking.

"Don't do this," he pleaded softly.

"Now!" she ordered, shooting over his shoulder.

He shuddered and tossed it to her.

#278 – The Emptiness of the End (4.9.19)

The emptiness of the end sat heavy in her stomach. She had waited all these months to be present when one of the packages was delivered.

Boris never spoke of the deliveries or the practices connected to what whatever he was receiving, but Ramos assured her that everything he claimed was true, that Boris could bring them power beyond comprehension if she were to acquire just one of the famed packages.

She arrived at Ramos's building and parked in the garage. After a moment she climbed out of her car and headed for the entrance, wondering what the future held.

Made in the USA
Lexington, KY
20 December 2019